'I'm digging you out of bankruptcy. I'll settle the overdraft and pay off any outstanding debts you might have.'

'Why would you do that?' she asked, her mouth suddenly bone-dry. 'What possible reason could you have for doing that?'

'I have a very good reason,' he said evenly.

A flutter of apprehension settled deep in her stomach. Here comes the fine print, she thought to herself: his conditions. 'And that is?' She managed to get the three words past the stiff line of her mouth.

His dark eyes held hers for a lengthy period before he finally spoke. 'I want you to have my baby.'

Melanie Milburne says: 'I am married to a surgeon, Steve, and have two gorgeous sons, Paul and Phil. I live in Hobart, Tasmania, where I enjoy an active life as a long-distance runner and nationally ranked top ten Master's swimmer. I also have a Master's Degree in Education, but my children totally turned me off the idea of teaching! When not running or swimming, I write, and when I'm not doing all of the above I'm reading. And if someone could invent a way for me to read during a four-kilometre swim I'd be even happier!'

Recent titles by the same author:

HIS INCONVENIENT WIFE

THE BLACKMAIL PREGNANCY

BY
MELANIE MILBURNE

Lynne,
Happy reading,
kind regards Melanie Milburne
Melanie

MILLS & BOON®

Dedicated to my husband Steve—love you to pieces

First published in Great Britain 2004
Harlequin Mills & Boon Limited,
Eton House, 18-24 Paradise Road, Richmond, Surrey TW9 1SR

© Melanie Milburne 2004

ISBN 0-263-83748-3

Set in Times Roman 10½ on 11½ pt.
01-0604-49514

Printed and bound in Spain
by Litografia Rosés, S.A., Barcelona

CHAPTER ONE

'IF YOU don't nail this deal, Cara, we're sunk.'

Cara stared at her business partner in shock.

'What do you mean "sunk"?' she asked, her palms moistening in mild panic.

Trevor flapped his hands in the air theatrically as he answered, 'Kaput, *finito*, washed up.'

She swallowed the lump of fear in her throat as she met his troubled gaze across the desk.

'But we're doing all right,' she said. 'You said so only last month at our planning meeting. And with the Pritchard account due any day now—'

Trevor shook his head.

'I had a meeting with the accountant this morning. Our business loan is stretched to the limit and the paltry Pritchard pennies won't even cover this week's interest, let alone next month's. That's why the Rockcliffe account is so crucial. We literally can't survive without it.'

Cara automatically stiffened at the mention of that name. Tiny feathers of fear tickled the length of her spine as she brought its owner's dark features to mind.

'Why me?' she asked after a lengthy silence, her skin still prickling in apprehension.

'Because you're the one he asked for, darling,' Trevor's tone was full of affront as he inspected his perfectly manicured nails. 'He insisted on you handling the whole account. Quite homophobic of him, I thought. But then you'd know all about that since you were once married to him.'

Cara's eyes gave little away, but inside she felt as if her stomach was unravelling.

'It was a long time ago, Trevor,' she said as dispassionately as she could. 'Seven years, in fact. I hardly even remember what he looks like. Probably got a paunch by now,
and a bald patch the size of a lawn,' she added for effect.

'Perhaps that's why he asked for you.' He grinned boy-
ishly. 'He might want to refresh your memory a bit.'

She gave him a reproving look.

'I'm sure there's nothing wrong with Byron Rockcliffe's
memory,' she said. 'It's his motives that worry me.'

'Motives?' Trevor's eyes widened expressively. 'Who
gives a fig about his motives? He's doing our business a
favour by engaging your services. Think of it! A harbourside mansion in Cremorne. Carte blanche, no questions
asked.'

'It sounds too good to be true,' she cautioned. 'I'd prefer
to see the fine print before I commit myself.'

'It's too late for that. I've already committed us—I mean
you.' He gave her a shame-faced look and continued,
'Sorry, pet, but I had to do it. I couldn't see all that money
going to someone else. You know what they say about looking a gift horse in the mouth.'

'Yes,' she said, getting to her feet and reaching for her
portfolio. 'I do know what they say, and you'd do well to
remember it. A horse's age is commonly assessed by the
length of its teeth. You have only to insist on the horse's
mouth being opened to see if what you're getting is really
a good deal.'

'I'm not sure it would have gone down too well if I'd
asked Byron Rockcliffe to open his mouth for me to peer
in.' Trevor chuckled. 'Perhaps I'll leave that to you.'

Cara gave him a fulminating look as she opened the office
door to leave.

'If I don't show up for work tomorrow it will be your
entire fault. You've put me in over my depth and I'm holding you totally responsible.'

'If you don't show up for work tomorrow I'll assume Byron Rockcliffe has talked you back into his bed,' Trevor said with a wolfish grin. 'He sounds so deliciously male. Mmm…such a waste.'

Cara turned on her heel and shut the door on her partner's teasing expression.

'Good luck!' Trevor's voice called from inside.

She didn't answer; she needed more than luck to get through the next hour or so. She needed a miracle.

The offices of Rockcliffe and Associates were huge even by Sydney standards. Cara took the shiny lift to the nineteenth floor, her heart beating a steady tattoo in her chest at the thought of seeing her ex-husband again.

The lift stopped on the thirteenth floor to let some people in and she wondered if it was some sort of omen. She pressed herself to the back of the stainless steel and mirrored walls and tried to concentrate on getting her breathing under some sort of control.

The lift stopped three more times, prolonging the agony, and she stared at the illuminated numbers above her head as if they were a countdown to disaster… Fifteen, sixteen, seventeen, eighteen…nineteen.

The doors pinged open and she jerked upright. Another wall of mirrors faced her as she stepped out. She looked at her reflection as if seeing it for the first time. Her mid-brown hair with its blonde highlights was falling from its clasp, her cheeks were flushed as if she'd just run up the nineteen floors, and the dark blue business suit she'd thrown on this morning shrieked off-the-peg. It was two seasons old and she'd lost weight since she'd bought it.

The blonde receptionist, however, was armoured with Armani and a heady perfume to match. Cara approached the arc of the front desk with a resentful trepidation.

'I have an appointment with Mr Rockcliffe,' she said in a voice that sounded distinctly rusty. 'At three p.m.'

The receptionist glanced at the appointment file on the computer screen in front of her.

'Ms Gillem?'

'Yes,' Cara answered.

'He's running a little behind.' The receptionist lifted a clear blue gaze from the screen to meet Cara's hazel one. 'If you don't mind waiting…'

'How much behind?' Cara interjected in irritation.

Now that she was here she wanted it over. She didn't want to be cooling her heels in his reception area under the catwalk gaze of his latest flavour of the month.

'Twenty minutes?' The blue eyes held no trace of apology. 'Maybe thirty.'

Cara took a steadying breath.

'I'll wait.'

Forty-three minutes later Cara heard the buzz of the intercom and buried her head back in the magazine she'd been pretending to read. Her heart thumped and her fingers shook as she turned the next page.

'Ms Gillem?' The receptionist's cool voice lifted Cara's head from the article on off-the-road four-wheel driving.

'He'll see you now,' she said. 'It's the first door on your right down the hall.'

Cara got to her feet, put the magazine down amongst the others and made her way down the hall on legs that threatened to give way beneath her. The hand she lifted to knock on the door marked 'Byron Rockcliffe' was visibly trembling, but she straightened her back and waited for his command.

'Come in.'

His deep voice washed over her in waves as she turned the doorknob. Her eyes searched for him as soon as the door was open, and found him seated casually behind his gargantuan desk. She was at an immediate disadvantage, as his broad shoulders blocked the afternoon light slanting in from the windows behind his desk. Although most of his face was in shadow, she could somehow sense his expression. She knew it would be mocking, sardonic, unaffected, while she stood before him like a reprimanded schoolgirl, her knees threatening to break the cool silence with their attempt to knock against each other.

'Cara.'

One word. Two syllables. Four letters.

'Byron.'

So formal. So coldly formal.

'Have a seat.'

She sat.

He leant back in his chair and surveyed her face for interminable seconds.

'Would you like a drink? Coffee? Something stronger?' he asked.

She shook her head and tightened her grasp on the portfolio she had clutched to her chest.

'Nothing, thank you. I'd prefer it if we were to get straight down to business.'

He reached for a pen, twirling it in his hand as his dark chocolate gaze met and held hers.

'Ah, yes,' he said, putting the gold pen down. 'The business. How's it going, by the way?'

'Excuse me?' Her tone was wary.

'Your business.'

'Fine.'

Even in shadow she could see the sceptical quirk of one dark brow.

'Fine?'

She swallowed and clutched her folder a little closer, as if it would protect her from the heat of his penetrating gaze.

'I'm sure you know I wouldn't be here if it were fine,' she said in a cold, almost detached voice.

'Wild horses wouldn't have dragged you?' he quipped.

'I thought Melbourne was your stamping ground,' she said.

'I've expanded,' he said. 'Business is booming.'

'Congratulations.' Her tone was anything but congratulatory.

'Thank you.'

'Trevor informed me of your request,' she said into the tight silence that had fallen between them. 'I can't imagine why you insist on me doing the work. Trevor is the creative brains behind our decorating business.'

'Your tendency to undersell yourself hasn't faded, I see,' he commented idly. 'How is your mother, by the way?'

'She's dead.'

Cara felt a faint glimmer of satisfaction at his reaction. Her simple statement had jerked him upright in his chair.

'I'm sorry,' he said. 'I hadn't heard.'

She shrugged her slim shoulders dismissively.

'It was a very private funeral.' Her voice was flat and unemotional. 'My mother had few friends.'

'How long ago?'

'Three years,' she said. 'It was very…quick.'

'Cancer?'

'No.' She met his dark gaze briefly. 'Complications after simple surgery.'

'It must have been a terrible shock for you.'

Cara rolled her lips and lamented the absence of lipstick. Ironic, really, that the absence of lipstick was more important to her than the demise of her mother.

'One moves on,' she said dispassionately.

'One does,' he replied, watching her steadily.

'So.' She swivelled her chair so that she was on a level with his dark eyes. 'Let's get down to business. Trevor said the property is in Cremorne. Does it have a harbour view, or is it—?'

'I'll take you there this afternoon,' he interjected.

'I can make my own way there,' she put in hastily.

'As you wish.'

Cara bit her lip. This was all wrong. She didn't feel at all like a person who laid down colour sheets and furniture brochures for the client's appraisal. She felt inadequate and on edge, as if the floor beneath her was going to be ripped out from under her.

'I need to go over colour schemes,' she said. 'I need to get some idea of layout, and—'

'I've got the plans here.' He reached towards a black shiny briefcase on one end of the large desk. He handed a sheaf of papers to her. 'All the specifications are there.'

She glanced down at the papers in her hands.

'What's the date of completion?' she asked.

'October first.'

'That's not a lot of time.'

'A month,' he said. 'Long enough.'

She lifted her eyes to his.

'Most furniture manufacturers require at least six to eight weeks' notification—fabric availability and so on.'

'So choose ones that only take a month,' he suggested.

'But—'

'Do it,' he said. 'I'm sure you of all people can pull a few strings to bring it about.'

Cara swallowed her answering retort and instead focused on the plans on her lap. The intricate architectural drawings blurred in front of her; it was like trying to read an ancient script with no prior knowledge of the language. She felt her nerves tightening in the back of her neck as she struggled to make sense of what was usually second nature to her. How swiftly he had unsettled her! She'd gone from a professional, highly skilled interior designer to a jittery mess in the space of a few minutes.

'I'll need some time to think about this,' she said, after another heavy silence. As she lifted her head she felt the clash of his dark gaze on hers.

'How much time?'

'A day or two—maybe three,' she answered, recalling her interminable wait for him in Reception.

He seemed to give her response some thought.

'All right,' he said at last. 'You have three days. I'll meet you at your office at twelve noon on Friday, but I want no further delays.'

'What exactly is the hurry on this?' she asked. 'You surely know enough about the business to realise a good job takes time?'

He tossed aside the pen he'd been clicking.

'I wish to move into the house as soon as possible. As it is, I've been at a hotel for three weeks and I'm getting a little impatient with all the stalling.'

'This is *your* house?' She looked at him in shock. 'You're going to live there?'

He nodded.

'But...but you live in Melbourne,' she said in rising panic. 'What about your family? And your business?'

'I decided it was time for a change.'

She took one deep swallow, hoping he couldn't see the way his words had unsettled her.

'The telephone directory is full of interior designers crying out for work,' she said, disguising her inner turmoil with an even tone. 'Why me?'

'Why not you?'

'Because there are so many more talented designers than me, that's why.'

'But I want you.'

Four simple words, but somehow she sensed a double

meaning in them. She sat on the edge of her seat, her hands clamped down on her knees to keep them from trembling in reaction.

'I'm flattered, of course,' she said without sincerity.

He got to his feet and his face came out of the shadows. Cara felt her breath trip in her throat at his sheer height and presence. His six feet five to her five feet seven had always been slightly intimidating, and now it was even more so. His dark straight hair was cut short and smoothed into place with styling gel. His clean-shaven jaw was already developing an evening shadow. The soft skin of her cheeks tingled in remembrance of the feel of his masculine skin rasping along hers. His mouth was set in a grim line, as if he was no longer in the habit of smiling. She mentally recalled his smile; it had been the first thing she'd noticed all those years ago: straight, even white teeth, and lips that curved upwards, sending crinkles of amusement to the corner of his chocolate eyes. Those eyes held no trace of such laughter now.

'You've changed your hair.'

Cara was knocked out of her silent reverie at his words. She got to her feet and self-consciously tucked a strand of blonde highlighted hair back behind her ear.

'Yes.'

She reached for the plans, but her hands fumbled picking them up and she watched as they slipped from her nervous grasp to lie in disarray on the floor. She bent down to retrieve them, but Byron had already swooped and was gathering them up. Cara reached for the last paper at the same time he did, her fingers touching his briefly. She pulled her hand away as if she'd been stung and got awkwardly to her feet.

She could feel his eyes on her and it made her angry that she couldn't get through this meeting without falling apart. She was sure he was enjoying her discomfiture. She was almost certain he'd engineered the whole enterprise. But why? He hadn't seen her in seven long years. What could he possibly want with her now?

The intercom buzzed and Cara let out her halted breath as he moved to the desk, her heart fluttering like an injured bird in her chest.

The cool, clear tones of the receptionist filled the silence. 'Byron, Mr Hardy is here to see you.'

'Thank you, Samantha.'

Cara gathered up her things and wondered what he called her in private. Would it be Sam, or Sammie? Grinding her teeth, she put the plans in her portfolio, resentment rising with every second.

'I won't be long,' he said. 'Please take a seat; I'll get Sam to bring you some coffee.'

'No, I must—' She looked up to protest but he'd already left the office.

Cara had no choice but to put her things back down and wait for him. Indignation fuelled along her veins at his over-bearing handling of her—as if she had nothing better to do with her time than play musical chairs in his suite of offices.

She ignored the chair she'd perched on earlier and, checking over her shoulder, approached the desk. His leather office chair still held the impression of his muscled thighs and she tore her eyes away from it. She didn't want to think about those thighs entwined with hers, his hair-roughened legs scraping along the smooth flesh of her own as he...

She swung away to inspect his desk. It was crafted out of Tasmanian myrtle, the rich red hues of the timber creating a type of warmth that made her want to reach out and touch it.

There was a photograph on the right-hand side of his computer console and before she could stop herself she picked it up and looked at it.

The Rockcliffe family were all there, with their various

partners—two of whom she didn't recognise—and gathered around them like trophies were six small children. Cara examined the features of each individual child and saw a little bit of Byron in each of them. An ache settled somewhere almost unreachable inside her, and she put the photograph down just as the office door reopened.

Byron's gaze swept over her standing behind his desk.

'I see you've reacquainted yourself with the family.' His tone was dry.

Cara stepped away from the desk with a guilty flush.

'That's quite some stud you've got happening down there,' she said in a voice that belied the true state of her feelings. 'Tell me, Byron, which children are yours?'

His eyes hardened momentarily. Cara prepared herself mentally for his reply, hoping it wouldn't hurt too much to hear how he was the father of one or two of those beautiful little faces in the photograph, not to mention the pain of finding out which of the young women was his new wife.

'None,' he stated flatly.

It took Cara a while for his one-word reply to sink in.

'None?'

'None.'

He took the chair she'd been sitting in earlier and propped one ankle across his knee in a casual pose. Cara envied his calm as he sat and watched her like an eagle, circling way above its prey, patiently waiting until it was finally time to swoop.

She couldn't hold his gaze. She absently fiddled with a paperclip on his desk, trying to frame the question that tore at her insides like rough claws. But before she could ask he asked one of his own.

'Any regrets, Cara?'

'What do you mean?' She glanced towards him briefly, not trusting herself to linger too long on his face. She didn't want him to see the pain in her eyes, the deep pang of regret and self-recrimination that was nearly always reflected there.

'Choosing your career over motherhood. Tell me, has it been as fulfilling as you anticipated?'

The paperclip pricked her finger and she let it drop back in the tray with an audible 'ping'.

'Of course,' she answered without meeting his gaze.

She could tell he didn't believe her.

'I love my job,' she said to cover the silence. 'And Trevor is fun to be around. He's so creative, inspiring me to do things I haven't done before.'

'Like go bankrupt?' he put in neatly.

She flashed him a resentful glare.

'Things are tight just now, but I'm sure we'll get out of it.'

'Your confidence does you credit,' he said. 'But from what I've gathered so far, things are very much on the downhill run.'

'That's not true!' Her denial was overdone but she couldn't stop herself in time. She just couldn't allow him to gloat over her failure. Her pride wouldn't cope. She wouldn't cope.

'Did Trevor tell you the bank is threatening to foreclose on your business loan?' he asked.

Panic rose in her throat and she swallowed it down with difficulty.

'I...'

'And that unless your cashflow increases dramatically everything you've put into the business will be lost, as well as any assets you might have accumulated over the past seven years?' He paused for effect. 'I trust you do have some sort of asset base?'

'Of course I do!' She glared at him angrily. 'Not that it's any of your business.'

'I'm making it my business.'

His statement held a trace of implacability about it that totally unnerved her. She released her clenched fists with an effort. She held on to the back of his office chair for support but it offered little; her fingers were trembling and the chair shifted under their feeble grasp.

'Wh…what do you mean?'

He waited until her eyes had returned to his to answer.

'I'm digging you out of bankruptcy. I'll settle the overdraft and pay off any outstanding debts you might have.'

'Why would you do that?' she asked, her mouth suddenly bone dry. 'What possible reason could you have for doing that?'

'I have a very good reason,' he said evenly.

A flutter of apprehension settled deep in her stomach. Here comes the fine print, she thought to herself: his conditions.

'And that is?' She managed to get the three words past the stiff line of her mouth.

His dark eyes held hers for a lengthy period before he finally spoke.

'I want you to have my baby.'

CHAPTER TWO

'You're out of your mind!' Cara threw the words at him in disbelief. 'You surely can't be serious?'

'Deadly serious.'

'But...' She ran her tongue over her parched lips agitatedly. 'But why? Why me?'

'As I said earlier, you're the one I want.'

She gaped at him with a combination of incredulity and dread.

'But why now?' she asked in desperation. 'Why now, after all this time?'

He got to his feet and she fought against the instinct to shrink behind his desk. He didn't approach her, but his eyes were like diamond chips as he stood watching every nuance of her expression.

'I'm the only one left in my family without children. I'm thirty-six years old and I want to look my own son or daughter in the eyes, not just those of my nieces and nephews.'

'But there are any number of women out there who would jump at the chance,' she croaked. 'With your sort of money you could even pay someone to do it, for God's sake!'

'I am paying someone to do it,' he said.

'Not me, you're not.' She shook her head. 'No way.'

She brushed past him to pick up her bag, but his hand snaked out and caught her, bringing her up short. She was suddenly much too close to him—too close to breathe, too close to think, too close to escape.

'Think about it, Cara.' His voice was gravelly. 'You can have it all. You can still have your career—my money will re-establish it.'

She tested his hold but it was firm. She met his eyes but they were implacable, determined. She felt cornered, like a small animal in a carefully constructed snare, all the tiny wires pulling against her resisting flesh.

'Don't do this to me, Byron,' she choked. 'Surely you don't hate me this much?'

He took his time answering and Cara felt the warmth of his breath on her face as he stood so close to her. Her traitorous body was already leaning towards him, looking for him, as if searching for her missing link.

'I don't hate you any more,' he said in a flat tone. 'I don't feel anything where you're concerned. I know what I want and I want you to be the one to give it to me.'

'But why?' she asked again. 'Is this some sort of sick seven-year plan for revenge?'

He shook his head, his hand still hard on her wrist.

'Not at all. As I told you, I've come to a certain point in my life where I want to achieve certain things. I don't want to be too old to enjoy my children. Nor do I want to wake up on the morning I turn forty and think—Oh, my God, I forgot to have kids! Don't you think about that sometimes, Cara?'

'Never,' she lied. 'I never think about it.'

'Well, I do,' he said. 'I think about it constantly. My three siblings are all younger than me and they all have children. Felicity is having her second in five weeks or so.'

Cara thought of Byron's younger sister in the last stages of pregnancy and swallowed deeply.

'Please don't ask this of me,' she pleaded with him. 'I'm not the right person. I don't have what it takes.'

'You do, but you just won't admit it. Deep down inside, where the real Cara is buried, you want the same thing I want. God knows I tried to get you to see it seven years ago, but failed. I'm not letting this opportunity pass without another attempt.'

'This is so cold-blooded!' she railed. 'How can you even think of bringing such a scheme about? It's inhuman. It's despicable, it's—'

'Nevertheless, it's what I want.'

'And what you want you automatically get?'

'Sometimes. Not always. But this time I'm counting on it.'

'Well, Byron, you've counted all wrong, because I'm not playing the game. Go find yourself another incubator—this one's not for sale.'

She wrenched herself out of his grasp and threw herself towards the door. She got to the lift and stabbed at the button, almost falling over in shock when immediately the doors pinged open. The lift whooshed down to the ground floor before the colour had returned to her face. She stepped out onto the busy city street and lost herself amongst the milling crowds, all the while trying to make some sense of the last hour.

Byron was a stranger to her now. Gone was the easy-going young man who'd swept her off her feet with one quick smile. In his place was a man determined to bring about his own agenda, no matter what it cost. She could only see it as a plan for revenge—but why had he waited so long to activate it? Had he been biding his time, waiting until she was truly vulnerable to swoop down and capture her?

'Trevor.' Her voice was ragged as she clutched the mobile to her ear. 'Tell me what the hell's going on.'

'Sweetie.' Her partner's tone was placating. 'You sound distracted. Didn't the meeting with Lord Byron go so well?'

'Lord is right,' she answered wryly. 'If anyone has a god complex it's Byron Rockcliffe.'

'I take it he's calling the shots?'

'More than you realise.' She stalled for breath before she

asked, 'Trevor, why didn't you tell me how bad things really were?'

'I didn't want to worry you,' he said. 'You've been down the last couple of months, and—'

'Trevor! I've been "down" for years, let's be honest. Why didn't you tell me?'

'I feel it's my fault,' he confessed awkwardly. 'I've pushed you along with my "creative genius", as you so fondly call it, but I haven't stopped to consider the risks. Now, I'm afraid, you're paying the price for that oversight.'

'I'm not paying any price,' she reassured him. 'Byron is over the top. I'm not doing what he wants.'

There was an ominous silence at the end of the line.

'Trevor?'

'Listen, Cara,' his tone was resigned. 'We have no choice. We're going belly-up without his help, and I can't call in any more favours to see us through. Just do what he says and let's get on with it. Surely it can't be that hard to decorate his castle and move on?'

'Harder than you know,' she said hollowly.

'If you need any advice, you know where I am,' he offered.

In spite of her troubles she had to laugh.

'Somehow, Trev, I don't think I'll be calling on you for help,' she said.

'Well, if you do, you know the number. Did I tell you I've got a hot date tonight?'

'No—with whom?'

'Antonio.'

'I thought he was on the back boiler?'

'I've been rethinking the whole issue. Better to have loved and left than never to have loved at all.'

'That's not quite how that saying goes,' she said with a wry twist to her mouth. 'But have a good time. I'll see you in the morning.'

* * *

Cara spent the next three days going through the books to see for herself how bad things really were. She met with the accountant and the bank manager, but the writing was well and truly on the wall—in neat and very precise figures. The bank manager was apologetic but realistic. He referred to the recent recession and advised her to accept the very generous financial help being offered; it was either that or declare herself bankrupt.

She left the bank in turmoil, blaming herself for not keeping a closer watch on things. Trevor was right; she had been down for the last couple of months—more than usual. Her twenty-ninth birthday was rapidly approaching and she hated her birthday. It reminded her of all she'd missed out on as a child.

She'd not long returned to the office when Trevor announced Byron's arrival. Cara glanced at her watch, her stomach freefalling in alarm. She hadn't heard from him since Tuesday afternoon, when she'd thrown his offer with its conditions in his face. She'd been pretending to herself that all of this was going to simply disappear. However, each morning she'd woken despairingly to the sickening realisation that this wasn't just a bad dream.

'Cara.'

She looked up to see him standing in the door of her office, his tall frame taking up much of the space. Any thoughts she'd had about making a timely escape were lost in the maelstrom of feeling that assailed her at seeing him once more.

He was dressed in a charcoal-grey business suit, which she assumed would be worth more than the contents of her entire current wardrobe. His shirt was white and his tie patterned in black, with tiny flecks of carmine. He looked fabulous.

She got up on unsteady legs and greeted him formally.

'Mr Rockcliffe, I—'

'Cara.' His deep voice cut her off. 'Let's drop the formalities, shall we? This is you and me, remember?'

She tore her eyes away from the chocolatey depths of his and instead concentrated on the knot of his tie.

'Byron, I don't wish to be rude, but I think we should stop this right here and now. Your...your offer to help is a very generous one, but I'm afraid I can't meet the terms.'

She saw his throat move up and down in a swallow and lifted her eyes slightly. He was frowning at her darkly, the line of his mouth hard.

'So you'd rather lose everything you own in the world rather than resume a temporary relationship with me?'

'Temporary?' Cara blinked at him uncomprehendingly.

'Of course temporary,' he said. 'You wouldn't want it any other way, would you?'

'I... No, of course not,' she said, looking away.

'Well, then,' he continued. 'Let's look at your options. You can come with me now, or you can ask me to leave. It's as simple as that.'

Cara couldn't speak. Thoughts were tumbling about her brain like clothes in a dryer. One thought kept tangling around the others until her head started to pound with the effort of keeping control of it.

'What's it to be, Cara?' he asked. 'Bankruptcy is no picnic. It's like a scar that has to be worn for the rest of your financial life.'

She knew all about scars. How intuitive of him to use that analogy! She so wanted to resist his offer, but a vision of the balance sheets swam before her eyes. She imagined herself trying to approach a bank for a loan in the future. It would be hopeless; she'd be considered a risk through no fault of her own other than naïvety.

In an attempt to escape the past she'd thrown everything into her career. She'd clawed her way through her course with high distinctions, finding solace in restoring older houses to their former glory. She'd decorated new houses to offset the wonderful designs that came across her desk, using to advantage every colour, every fabric and drape to make a lasting impression. Now all her hard work was going to go to waste unless she agreed to one small condition. Not so small, she reminded herself. Not small at all.

'Cara?'

She looked up at him once more, her throat tight with emotion.

'Could...could I see the house first?'

His brow furrowed into an even deeper frown.

'Why?'

She swallowed the restriction in her throat before answering.

'I'd like to see the house, that's all.'

'So you can weigh up the benefits?' His voice was hard with cynicism.

She turned away from the dark glitter of his eyes.

'I no longer make hasty, emotionally driven decisions,' she said in a cold, detached tone. 'I like to see things from several angles first.'

'Wise of you,' he commented, watching her closely.

She schooled her features into impassivity and reached for her handbag.

'Shall we go?'

The house was huge. Cara took a deep breath as Byron opened the front door and she stepped into the large foyer before him. A magnificent wrought-iron balustrade staircase swept the path of her eye upwards to the landing above where bright sunlight shafted through tall windows. The creamy marble floors in the living areas were interspersed with a toning plush crème carpet, creating added warmth.

She so wanted to do this house! It had an atmosphere like no other she'd ever been in.

'What do you think?' Byron spoke from behind her right shoulder.

She turned to face him, her eyes wide and expressive.

'It's…breathtaking.'

'Come and look at the view,' he said, leading her to the nearest window overlooking Neutral Bay.

She looked down on to the marina, beyond that to Kirribilli, and watched as the sunlight caught the mast of a passing yacht.

'From the master bedroom you can see Shell Cove,' he said into the silence.

'It's lovely, Byron.' She turned to him once more. 'It's the most beautiful house I've ever seen.'

'Praise indeed.'

She couldn't distinguish his tone. His expression was masked, as if he didn't want her to see what he was really thinking. She looked into his eyes, looking for reassurance. She found none. His eyes were like cold, deep pools—unfathomable, unreachable.

She moved away from the window and stepped down into the sunken lounge, her footsteps echoing along the floor. A large open fireplace took up almost one wall, and she imagined cosy evenings curled up on comfortable leather sofas, watching the flickering flames.

She was startled out of her reverie by the sound of Byron's approach. She swung away from the fireplace and headed for the kitchen, uncomfortable with being in the same room as him for too long.

'The kitchen, as you can see, has already been decorated.' Byron spoke from his leaning position against the doorframe.

'It's very nice,' she offered, running a hand across the black gleam of the granite countertop.

Stainless steel appliances added to the modern effect, and she knew she would have chosen exactly the same. She wondered if he'd chosen the design himself, or if perhaps his sister Felicity had helped him.

'I thought it would be best to get a head start on this. You can choose the colours for the rest of the house—the carpets and furniture and drapes and so on. Do whatever you think. I won't balk at the price.'

Cara's hand fell away from the smooth countertop as he stepped towards her.

'Byron, I—'

He cut off her speech with a long lean finger pressed gently but firmly against the soft swell of her lips.

'No, Cara,' he said softly. 'I don't want to hear your final decision yet.'

Her eyes communicated her distress.

'You haven't made up your mind, I can tell,' he continued, his dark eyes never once leaving her face. 'But you're sorely tempted—aren't you, Cara?'

She tried to shake her head, but couldn't move under the caress of his finger, tracing the line of her bottom lip on a path of rediscovery that sent tremors of feeling to her curling toes and back.

'You want the house but you haven't quite made up your mind about all that comes with it, have you?'

She opened her mouth to speak, but the words wouldn't come out.

'I'll give you until the end of the weekend to decide,' he said, stepping away from her. 'But that's all. On Sunday night I want your final answer.'

She felt cold without his warm body so close to hers. Her mouth felt dry and overly sensitive, and she ran her tongue over her lips and tasted where his finger had been.

'All right,' she said in a voice she hardly recognised.

He lifted his dark brows slightly, as if surprised by her acquiescence.

'Good,' he said. 'Come and I'll show you the garden. I think you'll like it.'

What was not to like? Cara thought as she followed him around the grounds. The crinkling surface of the lap pool glistened in the dancing sunlight and the fragrance of jasmine was heady in the air. Potted azaleas cascaded their bright blooms and the verdant expanse of lawn led down to a tennis court built on the lower terrace. The harbour sparkled in the distance and Cara breathed in the salty air and wished with every fibre of her being that she could turn back the clock.

As he came closer all the fine hairs on the back of her neck rose like antennae.

'Do you still play?' he asked, indicating the lush green of the tennis court as he stood beside her, his broad shoulder brushing against her.

She turned to look up at him, her throat suddenly dry.

'I haven't played in years.'

'Shame.' He looked down at her. 'You should take it up again. You were good. Damn good.'

Time seemed to stand still. Cara was almost certain she could hear the sound of children's laughter somewhere in the distance, but wondered if she'd just imagined it. The chirruping sparrows and the cooing doves on the lawn faded into the background as she lost herself in the deep, dark and mesmerising gaze of her ex-husband.

His head lowered towards hers, hesitated for an inestimable pause, then finished the distance with a soft press of his lips to hers. Her lips swelled in response. She could feel the tingle of their heightened sensitivity from that merest touch. His warm breath caressed her face before he pressed his mouth to hers once more—firmer this time, but only just.

A part of Cara demanded she step away from that tempting mouth. But an even bigger part of her overruled it. It was just a kiss, she reassured herself. Almost a kiss between strangers.

But there was nothing strange about Byron's mouth when he swooped a third time. Her mouth flowered open beneath his, just like one of the spilling azalea blooms at their feet. His tongue grazed her bottom lip and her fight was over before it had even truly begun. His tongue tangled with hers and she would have fallen if it hadn't been for the steel band of his arm coming around her to draw her into the hard wall of his body. She jolted against him in a combination of shock at his ready arousal and shame at her instant response to it. She wanted him. After seven long years she was his for the asking, and his mouth was responding to hers as if he knew it as well.

Cara felt the brush of his hand underneath her breast and ached for the cradle of his palm on her engorged flesh. He pulled her further into his body and her pelvis loosened at the feel of his hips grinding into hers. He was rock-hard, and even through the barrier of their clothes she could feel his scorching heat. Her secret place remembered and responded, moistening in preparation for the intimate invasion she'd spent seven years trying to expunge from her mind.

He lifted his mouth from hers and stepped away. Cara steadied herself by grasping the wrought-iron railing that divided the lap pool from the lawn. She brushed back her loosened hair with a hand that threatened to betray her outward composure.

'I'll be waiting in the car,' he said in a flat, emotionless tone. 'Take your time looking around. I have some phone calls to make.'

As he strode towards the side gate Cara stared after him until he disappeared from view. She ran her tongue over her swollen mouth and tasted him. Familiar, yet strange. Known but now unknowable.

She looked up at the big empty house and agonised over

what her decision would be on Sunday evening. She wasn't sure she had much say in the matter; the way her body was feeling had already decided for her. Did she have the strength to walk away from him a second time?

She went back through the house via the bathroom, to tidy herself before rejoining Byron at the car. She stared at her reflection in the mirror and was a little shocked by the wild, abandoned look in her hazel-flecked eyes. Passion burned in her gaze—a dormant passion now stirred into blistering life by just one kiss from a mouth that still hadn't once smiled at her.

CHAPTER THREE

BYRON was leaning against the car, listening to someone on the other end of his mobile phone, his eyes squinting slightly against the bright sunshine. Cara approached the car and he turned as if he sensed her behind him. He carefully avoided her eyes as he came around and opened the door for her. He finished the call and slid into the driver's seat, all without addressing a single word to her.

Cara wanted to break the silence but couldn't think of anything to say. What did one say to an ex-husband in these situations? I still love you after all these years? I made a mistake, the biggest mistake of my life, when I left you? Can we try again?

'No.'

'Did you say something?' His eyes flicked her way as he turned the wheel.

She hadn't realised she'd spoken out loud, so deep was her concentration on the past.

'No, nothing…'

He turned the car into the traffic before speaking again.

'I thought we could have lunch.' He glanced at the car clock. 'I have a client at two, but if we're quick we can grab a sandwich and a coffee somewhere.'

Cara didn't want to appear too desperate for his company, and wished she could invent two or three clients of her own, but the rest of her afternoon was unfortunately very free.

'I should get back to the office—'

'And do what?' He glanced at her again. 'Your business has ground to a halt. Is my company so distasteful to you that you can't even stomach the thought of sharing a simple meal with me?'

She flinched at the bitterness in his voice.

'No, of course not.' But even to her own ears her tone lacked conviction.

'No wonder you're balking at the suggestion of sharing my bed,' he ground out. 'Let alone bearing my child.'

Cara stared at her tightly clenched hands in her lap, and before replying waited until she had her emotions under some sort of control.

'Lunch will be fine,' she said at last. 'I don't have any other engagements.'

He drove to a café in Neutral Bay in stony silence. Cara looked at him once or twice, but his attention was on the traffic ahead. His normally smooth brow was deeply furrowed, the lines around his mouth tightly etched, as if he were only just managing to keep control of his anger. She knew he was angry with her. Seven years of anger separated them just as much as the issues that had caused the first rift.

She'd been adamant from their very first date that she had no intention of ever having children. She hadn't told him the real reason, but instead had grasped for the generally held assumption that young career-driven women had better things to do with their time than haunt some man's kitchen barefoot with a protruding belly. The fact that she hadn't at that point in her life had a career hadn't taken away the strength of her argument. But at twenty-two years old what truths of the world had she really known? She'd flitted from job to job, searching for something she had known was out there somewhere for her to devote herself to. But back then it hadn't yet appeared on the horizon.

It had taken the bitter divorce to propel her into the field of interior design. She'd immersed herself in her studies, trying to dull the throb of pain that just wouldn't go away.

And yet for all her efforts the pain was still there, waiting for a chance to break free of its bounds.

Byron parked the car and she joined him on the pavement outside the café. A waitress led them to a table shaded by a huge leafy tree and Cara sat down and stared at the menu sightlessly.

'Cara?'

She looked up and his eyes clashed with hers.

'What sort of coffee would you like?' he asked, indicating the hovering waitress.

'I'll just have a mineral water, please,' she told the waitress, who then moved to the next table.

She could feel Byron's speculative gaze on her and fidgeted with the hem of the tablecloth to distract her.

'What happened to the latte lady?' he asked.

She gave a shrug and examined the menu once more.

'She couldn't sleep.'

As she looked up and caught the tail-end of a small smile she wished she'd looked up earlier.

'Do you drink?'

'Alcohol, you mean?'

He nodded.

'Not any more.' She lowered her gaze once more and stared at a tiny crinkle in the tablecloth in front of her.

'Tell me about your mother, Cara.'

Cara stiffened. Schooling her features back into indifference was hard with him sitting so close. So close and yet so far.

'I don't wish to speak ill of the dead,' she countered, and was relieved when the waitress arrived with their drinks.

She drank thirstily and hoped he'd move onto another subject.

Once the waitress had left Byron spooned sugar into his cappuccino and stirred it thoughtfully. He'd been a little unprepared for seeing Cara again. He'd thought it would be easy. He'd breeze in and call the shots. But somehow something wasn't quite right. He'd been too young and inexperienced to see it before. He'd fallen in lust and then in love with an ideal—an ideal that had turned out to be a real woman with issues that just wouldn't go away. He could see that now. Hurt shone from her hazel eyes, hurt that he'd certainly contributed to—but not just him; he felt sure about that.

She'd never let him meet her mother. He wondered now why he hadn't insisted. Somehow Cara had always found an excuse: her mother was away visiting relatives, couldn't make it to the wedding, had the flu and wasn't seeing anyone. He hadn't pressed her about it. Anyway, her mother had lived in another state, so visiting had mostly been out of the question. He had spoken to Edna Gillem once on the telephone, and it still pained him to recall their conversation. It had well and truly driven the last nail into the coffin that had contained his short marriage.

With the wisdom of hindsight he could see the mistakes he'd made almost from the first moment he'd met Cara. She had been out with a group of friends whom he'd later referred to as 'the pack'. They had been like baying hounds, crying out for male flesh, and from the first moment he had seen Cara was in the wrong company. She'd looked scared, vulnerable in a way that had dug deeply at the masculine protective devices his father and grandfather before him had entrenched in his soul.

He'd taken her to one side to buy her a drink and one drink had led to another. He'd taken her to his apartment and she'd fallen asleep on his sofa. In three weeks she had been sleeping in his bed, and eight weeks later wearing his ring. He'd never slept with a virgin before, and it had taken him completely by surprise.

He often felt guilty when he recalled his actions of all those years ago. If only he'd taken his time, got to know her—the real Cara, not the shell she presented to the world. Maybe he wouldn't be sitting opposite her now, in a crowded café, with the pain of seven years dividing them. They could have had kids in school by now—kids with hazel eyes and light brown hair that wouldn't always do as it was told.

He stirred his coffee and took a deep draught, his eyes catching hers as she reached for her mineral water. What was she thinking? She looked so cool, so composed, but still he wondered...

'How are your parents?' she asked.

He gave his coffee another absent stir and Cara saw the hint of a small smile of affection briefly lift the corners of his mouth.

'They're fine. Fighting fit. Dad has taken up golf and Mum is part of a bridge club.'

'And your twin brothers and sister?'

He pushed his half-finished coffee aside and met her interested gaze.

'Patrick eventually married Sally, and they have five-year-old twins—Katie and Kirstie. Leon and Olivia now have three kids—Ben, seven, Bethany, five, and Clare is three. Fliss has two-year-old Thomas, and is apparently expecting a girl this time.'

Cara drained her glass and set it aside.

'And your business?' she added. 'It finally took off?'

'Like you would never believe,' he said, and then added with a rueful twist to his mouth, 'You should've hung around.'

She didn't respond. The waitress appeared with the sandwiches he'd ordered earlier, and she stared at the food set down before her and wondered how she'd ever force it down her restricted throat.

She'd never doubted he'd be successful as a property developer; he came from a long line of very successful moneyed men. What surprised her was how little that success had fulfilled him. She'd imagined him married, with the brood of kids he'd always wanted, but he was still single—and asking her to resume their relationship temporarily. She didn't understand him. Perhaps she never had.

Some endless minutes passed before either of them spoke.

'My parents send their regards,' Byron said. 'I was speaking to them last night.'

Cara met his eyes across the table and looked away again.

'Please send on my own. I've thought of them over the years.'

'What about me?' he asked after a tiny pause. 'Have you thought about me?'

She fidgeted with her napkin, ignoring the untouched food in front of her.

'A bit.'

'Just a bit?'

'A lot.'

He seemed satisfied with her answer and she instantly regretted saying anything that would make Byron think she was still hankering after him, like a lovelorn ex-wife who couldn't get her life back on track.

'Did Felicity finish her degree?' She asked the first question that came into her mind.

'With honours. We're very proud of her. She's the first Rockcliffe female to complete a doctorate. My mother got as far as her master's, but it took Fliss's determination and brilliance to lift the game that next notch.'

'I always thought she'd do it,' Cara said. 'She's got what it takes.'

'Evidently so have you,' he observed. 'That's an impressive degree hanging on your office wall.'

'It came at a high price.'

'But worth it, surely?' he asked. 'You've made your mark on Sydney's design intelligentsia.'

'But not on the bank manager.'

'No, but they're hard to please at the best of times.'

She felt a smile tug at her mouth.

'Trevor would be glad to hear you say that,' she said.

'Did you meet him at design school?'

She nodded. 'He was a friend of a friend—you know how it goes.'

'Have you got a boyfriend? A lover?'

Cara bent her head over her food, playing with the salad garnish. 'I can't see that it's any of your business. What about you?' She lifted her eyes gamely to his.

His dark gaze gave nothing away. 'Suffice it to say I'm in between appointments.'

Her heart squeezed at the thought of him involved with someone else, but she fought against revealing her feelings to him. It was none of her business who he slept with—now.

'So I take it your offer to me is some sort of stop-gap?'

'You might like to see it that way, but I prefer to see it as an investment in the future.'

'There's not much future for children without two loving parents,' she pointed out. 'Surely all children are entitled to at least that?'

'That's the ideal, of course, but life doesn't always go to plan. There are literally thousands of households headed by single parents. No one could say they're doing a substandard job; they're just getting on with it—bringing up the next generation as best they can.'

Cara toyed with her food, rearranging it without lifting any morsel of it to her mouth.

'Some do better than others,' she said, pushing her plate away.

Byron knew her statement was loaded but decided against pressing her. She looked tired, almost defeated, as if the world had been cast upon her slim shoulders. She was visibly sagging. Her eyes refused to meet his and her shoulders were slumped as if in surrender. He thrust his napkin aside and got to his feet.

'Come on. I'll take you back to your office.'

She was glad of the reprieve. She felt uncomfortable in his company and couldn't wait to be free of it so she could think clearly. Having him so near clouded her thoughts, ran them together—like a red T-shirt thrown amongst white washing.

He settled the bill and she allowed him to lead her by the elbow towards the car.

'I'll see you on Sunday,' he said when he left her outside her office. 'I'll pick you up from your home. Trevor gave me your address the other day.'

Cara waited until his car had disappeared down the street before she turned towards her office, her thoughts jumbled inside her head.

Trevor was waiting for her.

'How was it?'

'How was what?'

'The house,' he said in excitement. 'Was it everything and more?'

She gave him a vague smile and pushed past to go to the sanctuary of her office.

'It was that and more. I'm going to take the job and start work immediately. I've got a house—no, a mansion to fill with furniture, and only four weeks in which to do it.'

Trevor gave a whoop of delight.

'That's my girl!' he crowed. 'We're not going under!'

No, she thought. You're not going under—just me. And she closed her office door on his carefree smiling face.

Byron was right on time when he pulled up in front of her small rented apartment on Sunday evening. Cara had been watching from the window and now stood in the hall, waiting for his knock.

She opened the door and felt her stomach tilt at the sight of his tall frame before her. He was wearing dark trousers and a lightweight knit top that highlighted the breadth of his shoulders.

She had chosen to go casual as well. Her camel coloured pants teamed nicely with her black top, and her hair was loose for a change. She saw his eyes flick over her as she stood before him, his expression giving nothing away. She wanted to say hello, but instead reached for her bag, trying to cover her unease.

'I thought we might go somewhere quiet and discuss your decision over dinner,' he said as she followed him out to his car.

'Fine.'

One-word answers were all she could manage on the way to a little Italian restaurant in Glebe. Cara sat twisting the strap of her bag and wondered what he was thinking. Was he anticipating resuming their relationship tonight? Or would he wait until she'd finished the house?

They were seated with drinks and menus in front of them when Byron asked, 'Have you come to a decision?'

She looked up at him in alarm. Couldn't he at least wait until their food had been ordered?

'I meant about the food,' he added with a small tilt of his mouth as he noticed her troubled expression. 'You don't need to panic just yet.'

'I'm not panicking.'

'Yes, you are. I can feel your tension from here.'

'I'm not tense, I'm…I'm concentrating.'

'On what?'

'The menu.'

'What do you feel like?' he asked.

'What?'

He gave her another frustrated look.

'I'm still talking about the food.'

'I haven't had time to look,' she replied coolly. 'You keep badgering me with questions.'

'Sorry.' His apology was gruff as he returned to his own menu. 'I realise this isn't easy for you.'

'Are we still talking about food?' she asked.

His mouth twisted as he met her eyes across the table.

'No, not this time.'

The waiter appeared and asked for their order. Cara rattled off the first thing she'd seen under main courses and sat back and waited for Byron to relay his own preference. Once the waiter had bustled away she felt the full heat of Byron's gaze.

'So, what have you decided, Cara?'

'I'd hardly call it a decision,' she said with some resentment. 'You've made it very difficult for me to do anything else.'

'I made it difficult?' he asked with heavy irony. 'I wasn't the one who didn't take a decent look at the business end of things until it was too late to do anything. What world are you living in, Cara? You can't blame other people for your own mistakes—even if they were innocently made.'

She gave him a tight-lipped cold stare.

'Trevor is not an ideal business partner,' he continued.

'Why?' She threw the question at him crossly. 'Just because he's gay?'

'No,' he answered evenly. 'It has nothing to do with that. He hasn't got what it takes to run a business.'

'And neither do I?'

He reached for his glass of red wine and twirled it in his hand before responding.

'No. Your heart's not in the books—it's in the design end of things. I could see it in your eyes when you saw my house.'

He was right, but she wasn't going to let him enjoy that little victory.

'We can't all be highfliers like you, Byron,' she said. 'Trevor and I weren't educated in one of Victoria's most prestigious fee-paying schools. We don't have family money to back us.'

'You had my money. The divorce money.'

'It's expensive setting up an office,' she said. 'The computers and so on.'

He seemed to accept her answer and she inwardly sighed with relief.

'How soon can you get the house ready to live in?' he asked, unsettling her again.

'I…I've got a few ideas about furniture, but it could be weeks.'

'I told you a month—that's all.'

'It's not long enough.'

'Surely we can live in the house with the bare essentials?' he said. 'All we need is a bed and—'

'You expect me to live with you?' she asked in alarm.

'Of course. I thought you understood that.'

'But what about my apartment?'

'You call that shoebox an apartment?'

She gave him another cold, resentful glare.

'I would've thought you'd have the most sensational home after all those years in the business. Or is this yet another case of the plumber with a leaky tap?' he added when she didn't respond.

'I had other priorities. I'm hardly home, so it didn't seem important,' she said.

'Well, you can sell it, or rent it out for the time being. I want you to live with me at the Cremorne house and I want you to start tomorrow—furniture or no furniture.'

'Tomorrow?' Her eyes widened in panic.

'I'm signing on the dotted line tomorrow with your financial people. I expect you to fulfil your part of the contract.'

'I hardly call it a contract,' she ground out bitterly. 'More like a dictatorship.'

'Call it what you like. It's immaterial to me. I'm putting a lot of money in your business and I want some immediate returns on my investment.'

'You're sick,' she fired at him. 'How can you sit there and discuss this…this farce, so clinically?'

'Quite frankly, Cara, I don't really care what you think about me personally. I have a goal in mind, and this time not even you are going to stand in my way.'

'You definitely need help,' she muttered as she savaged her bread roll. 'I've never met anyone with such a big ego.'

'And I've never met anyone with a lesser one,' he countered neatly.

Cara's butter knife clattered against her plate as she looked away from his penetrating gaze. Fortunately the waiter appeared just then, with their food, and she was spared the right of reply. Not that she could think of one; he was right—she had no self-esteem, never had. Her mother had seen to that, right up to the very day she died.

She forced herself to eat at least some of the food set before her, even though her appetite had completely disappeared.

'You don't seem to be enjoying that,' Byron observed some minutes later. 'Would you like something else instead?'

She shook her head and forced another mouthful down.

'You look as if you're going to face a firing squad at dawn,' he said after another minute or two had elapsed. 'Relax, Cara. You might even enjoy it.'

A vision of their passion-locked bodies flitted unbidden into her mind and she lowered her head to her plate to disguise the heat she could feel coursing across her cheeks.

After a few painful minutes she pushed her plate away in defeat. She wiped her mouth on her napkin and caught the hard glint in his eyes.

'You'd do anything but talk to me, wouldn't you, Cara? Even force-feed yourself a meal you don't want so you don't have to speak to me.'

'I have nothing to say to you.'

'Nothing?'

'Nothing.'

'What about, How was it for you that day I left? Were you upset? That would be a good place to start.'

Her hands tightened in her lap but she didn't answer him.

'Or what about, Did you know I was pregnant when I left? That would make for a very interesting conversation, now, don't you think?'

Cara stared at him in abject horror, all the colour draining away from her face. His expression was clouded by anger, his dark eyes glittering dangerously with it, showing her that this was no time for denial. Without warning the moment of truth she'd quietly dreaded for seven years had finally caught up with her.

CHAPTER FOUR

SHE couldn't speak. Anguish tied her tongue and sent tremors of reaction to her very fingertips. They were already fizzing, as if her blood couldn't quite make the distance to them. She felt as if she would faint—hoped for it, in fact. How could she avoid the subject she dreaded the most?

'Let's get out of here.' Byron suddenly broke the heavy silence by getting to his feet and signalling to the waiter for the bill.

Cara got to her feet with considerably less agility. Her legs were shaking, her palms moist, and the rest of her body felt as if it had been clubbed.

Byron fixed the bill and led the way back to his car in silence. He unlocked the doors with a snap of the remote that sounded like a gunshot and she had to stop herself from flinching.

'Get in.'

His words were just as sharp, hitting her like bullets. She got in the car, glad that her legs didn't have to hold her upright any more. He started the car with a roar that indicated the depth of his anger. Although he'd hidden it well, he'd waited until she was lulled into a false sense of security and then struck her where she was most vulnerable.

He drove towards her apartment with a grim determination that did little to settle Cara's nerves. She had so much to say, but most of it could never be for his ears. He'd never understand the sort of decisions she'd had to make. The secrets she'd kept; the pain she'd hidden in order to survive.

He walked her to her apartment, all the while maintaining cold silence. She didn't know what was worse. Hearing him castigate her, bearing his stony silence or torturing herself with what she imagined he was thinking.

At the door of the apartment she turned to him, forcing herself to meet his diamond-hard gaze.

'Thank you for dinner.'

He seemed about to say something, but then changed his mind. He raked a hand through his dark hair and the lines around his mouth appeared to relax a little.

'Will you need some help packing?' he asked.

'No, I'll be fine. I don't have all that much to pack,' she answered in a subdued tone.

Byron watched as she unlocked the door and stepped through, hesitating, as if she wasn't sure if she wanted him to come in or not. He guessed not. He hadn't really intended to ask her that question tonight, but he'd been increasingly annoyed by her attitude towards him. She barely tolerated his presence and it irritated him. He had felt like shaking her out of her skin.

Her eyes, when they met his again, looked wounded, which instantly made him feel like the bad guy. How did she do that? He had every right to be furious with her. She had no right to play the injured innocent. No right at all.

'What time would you like me to be at Cremorne?' she asked.

Byron hunted her face for any sign of her composure cracking, but apart from that hurt look in her eyes there was none. She'd effectively shut him out once more, and apart from flaying her with his tongue right here and now there was little he could do but accept it for now. He'd bide his time and get the answers he was after—even if it took him months.

'In the evening's fine,' he answered, giving her a key.

He noticed she took it from him without touching his hand. That too made him angry. She'd have to get used to him touching her, because that was all he wanted to do—

from the moment he woke until he fell asleep at night. His body craved her. Being so close to her had stirred his desire to a persistent dull ache, and he wondered if she sensed it.

He turned to leave before he was tempted to do something about it then and there. He muttered a curt goodnight as he closed the door on her expressionless face.

Cara sagged against the wall once he'd gone, burying her face in her hands, slipping down until she found the floor.

She stayed up most of the night packing. She knew sleep was impossible, so continued on until her vision blurred. The last bag was packed and she stood up and looked around her tiny apartment. Three bags and a box wasn't much to show for her almost twenty-nine years, but then, she reflected ruefully, she had enough internal baggage to sink a container ship.

She sat and sipped a glass of water as she watched the moon make its way across the early morning sky until the brightness of the rising sun took over.

This was the first day of the rest of her life. She knew from this day on nothing could ever be the same. Seeing Byron again had torn her seeping wounds apart, and no matter how hard she tried she'd never be able to tie the ragged edges together again. She almost hated him for his cruelty. Almost, but not quite.

Cara spent some time at the office—more to fill in the day than because of any pressing work commitments. Trevor took one look at her shadowed eyes and whistled through his teeth.

'You're looking a bit the-morning-after-the-fight-before.'

She gave him a you-can-say-that-again look and flopped into her chair.

'I'm not even going to correct your misquote of that adage, because your version's far more accurate.'

He perched on the edge of her desk, his expression empathetic. 'Lord Byron giving you a hard time?'

'You could say that.' She gave a deep sigh. 'I'm moving in with him this evening.'

Trevor's eyes widened, his brows disappearing under his floppy fringe.

'Is that wise?'

She gave him an ironic look.

'No, but wisdom doesn't come into it, I'm afraid. It's a matter of do or be damned.'

'Is he forcing your hand?'

'Oh, I had a choice,' she said. 'Sort of.'

'I'm sorry, Cara,' he said. 'This is all my fault. It's not fair that you're being forced to pay the price.'

'Don't worry about it,' she reassured him. 'I'll be fine. Byron will soon tire of me. I'm what is commonly referred to by most men as "hard work".'

'You're not hard work,' he said. 'You're wounded. That's totally different.'

She gave him a small wry smile.

'Only you would see the difference.'

'I'm sure he will too, in time. Maybe you should be totally honest with him. He might understand more than you think,' he offered hopefully.

'Byron's not the understanding type. He's had life too good. What would he know about how the other half live? He's had everything handed to him on a plate—including me.'

'Do you still care for him?'

'I don't know what I feel,' she answered honestly. 'I've taught myself not to feel anything for so long I can't quite find the on switch any more.'

'It will come back if you give yourself some time. You need to let the dust of the past settle for a little longer, get some more perspective.'

'You should've been a counsellor, Trev,' she said. 'You've got all the answers.'

'No, I haven't.' He kissed the top of her head as he jumped down from her desk. 'I just know what the questions are.'

Cara drove towards Cremorne, her heart still heavy in her chest at what she was about to commit to. Byron was little more than a stranger to her now. How was she to simply slot back into his life as if nothing had happened? It would take all the acting ability she had to survive.

His car was in the large garage, and she parked in the space alongside it. Her run-down Mazda looked very out of place next to his Mercedes—but then, nearly everything about them was just as disparate.

He came to help her with her things and she felt a wave of self-consciousness wash over her as his eyes took in her tired-looking bags and the single cardboard box.

'Is that all?' he asked, tucking the third case under his arm.

'Yes.'

'What about your furniture?'

'I don't have any.'

He shouldered the front door open as he looked at her questioningly.

'You were renting?'

She nodded, brushing past him with her box against her chest like a shield. He followed her in and, still frowning, took her things up to the master bedroom.

Cara looked at the king-sized bed and put her box on the end of it, her heart beating an erratic tattoo in her chest. It was made up with caramel-coloured linen and white pillows with a matching caramel trim. Several plump cushions were propped up against the pillows. She wondered if he'd had it delivered that day. It unnerved her to think of him so eager to resume a physical relationship with her when her emotions were in such tatters. How could she keep herself under control with him storming her defences in such a way?

'There's a walk-in wardrobe through that door.' He pointed in its direction. 'The *en suite* is over there. I'll leave you to sort things out. I'll get a start on dinner.'

Cara sat on the huge bed and looked around the room. As master bedrooms went it was one of the biggest she'd seen. The soft cream of the walls toned perfectly with the bedlinen, and although the marble floor was bare she could already imagine the rugs she'd lay down.

She got off the bed to look out of the large windows. The view was spectacular: the night lights of the city twinkling in the distance, and just below a harbour cruiser sailed past the marina with its arc of decorative golden bulbs.

She unpacked her few things into the spacious walk-in wardrobe and wondered if she'd ever be in a position to have enough clothes to fill it completely. She tried to ignore the neat row of Byron's clothes hanging on the other side. She could pick up the faint smell of his aftershave clinging to his things and a host of memories assailed her. Almost without her volition she reached for one of his sweaters and buried her face in its folds, breathing in the scent of him lingering there.

She turned back to the task at hand and shut the door behind her once she'd finished. She wished she could close off the memories just as effectively.

She made her way downstairs with weary steps, her stomach tightening at the thought of the rest of the evening.

Byron was in the kitchen preparing some pre-cooked food. He looked up as she came in, his eyes sweeping over her assessingly.

'You look tired. Are you hungry?'

'Not really,' she answered truthfully.

'Didn't you sleep?'

She shook her head.

'Is the thought of being with me so torturous?' he asked with a flint-like edge to his tone.

She didn't answer. His mouth tightened as he placed a container in the microwave and she wondered if he were feeling the tiniest bit remorseful over the machinations that had led her here tonight.

'I'm going to engage a housekeeper,' he informed her coolly.

'But there's no furniture to dust,' she pointed out.

'There will be soon,' he said. 'We both work full time, this is a big house, and I don't want you to waste your energy on tasks that can be better outsourced.'

'When do you want me to start on your little project?' she asked with a hardened look in her eyes. 'I take it you'd like to get to the task at hand as soon as possible?'

His eyes met her challengingly.

'You fight me at every corner, don't you? Even though both of us really want the same thing.'

'You know nothing of my wants.'

'Don't I?' he asked. 'I wouldn't bet on that, if I were you.'

She spun away in anger, unable to look him in the eyes. The microwave pinged and she heard him rattle plates and cutlery behind her as he set their meal on the bench.

They ate in silence. Cara picked at the food and eventually pushed it aside, concentrating on her glass of water.

'You don't eat properly,' he said, flicking a glance towards her plate before returning his eyes to hers.

'Is there anything else you'd like to criticise while you're at it?' she asked. 'Is my hair not to your liking? Or perhaps you think my clothes are outdated and my thighs full of cellulite?'

He frowned and pushed his own plate away.

'I'm not criticising you, merely making an observation.'

'I don't like being observed.'

'I know that.'

'Then don't do it.'

'How am I supposed to get to know you if I don't observe you?' he asked.

'You don't need to get to know me,' she answered coldly. 'Your goal is to get me pregnant, remember? You don't need to know me at all to do that.'

He didn't offer a reply. Her face was stormy enough as it was; he didn't want to make things any worse than they were already.

She got to her feet, scooped up her plate, took it across the kitchen and thrust the barely touched contents into the garbage bin. She heard Byron come up behind her and turned away to give him room.

'Cara?'

She stopped, her back still rigid towards him.

'Don't do the Joan of Arc routine, OK?'

She turned to look at him, her expression bright with barely repressed anger.

'No one likes a martyr, and it won't help things between us if you persist in casting me in the role of the big bad guy,' he said.

'You put yourself in that role,' she said heatedly. 'I'm just the one dancing to your tune.'

'You haven't got the steps right so far.'

'What do you want me to do?' she flared at him. 'Do you want me to grovel at your feet in gratefulness at your magnanimous financial gesture?'

'No, of course not. I—'

'You have a nerve, Byron Rockcliffe.' She thrust a pointed finger at his chest before he could finish his sentence. 'You think you're so smart, calling all the shots now. You feel so powerful, with me stuck under your thumb like a moth on a toothpick. But I will never bend to your will, no matter how much you try to manipulate me. You can force me to do anything you like, but deep down you will always have to face the fact that I didn't come to you willingly. Can you live with that?'

His eyes burned into hers with an answering heat.

'Yes. I can live with that.'

It wasn't the answer she had been expecting. She stood stiffly before him, her eyes darting anywhere but in his direction.

'I've resigned myself to the fact that you are determined to cross me at every point, but I'm equally determined to break through your defences. You've been hiding for far too long; it's time you faced life head-on.'

'What would you know about life?' she retorted with cold sarcasm. 'You with your perfect family and a silver spoon stuck halfway down your throat since the moment you were born. What would you know?' Unexpected tears brightened her eyes and she turned away from his all-seeing gaze.

'I know enough to see you're carrying far too much baggage for a young woman of your age,' he said in a gentler tone. 'But you won't trust anyone enough to help you.'

She brushed at the tears in her eyes with an angry hand and faced him again, her cheeks hot, her bottom lip wobbling uncontrollably.

'Don't push me,' she warned him. 'Don't you dare push me.'

He sighed and rubbed his shadowed jaw with one hand in a gesture of helplessness.

'I don't know how to handle you in this mood,' he confessed.

'Leave me alone,' she said brokenly. 'I need some time alone.'

He came over to her and touched her gently on the shoulder, but she flinched away from his touch.

'Cara, this is—'

'Please.' Her tone was pleading. 'I just need some time alone.'

He sighed and left her standing against the countertop, her small frame shaking from trying to repress the sobs that threatened to overcome her.

Byron stood in the large lounge and stared out at the night-time view with unseeing eyes. He seriously wondered whether he had what it took to carry on. He began to see himself through her eyes and felt sickened by the way he'd engineered things to get his way, without stopping to think of the impact on her fragile emotions. He'd had a goal in mind and set out to achieve it; he hadn't allowed for her at all. But then, when had he ever allowed for their differences?

He thought back to the time when they had been together so briefly and realised with a sickening jolt just how much he'd railroaded her—first into sleeping with him and then into marriage. He hadn't given her time to think for herself. He'd acted in response to his own impulses and hadn't given her time to refuse him.

He left her for half an hour before tracking her down in the bedroom. He'd gone with a speech prepared, but when he saw her curled up on the big bed, her face turned into the pillow, he felt the words die in his throat.

She was curled up into a tight ball, her arms tucked into her stomach, her slim form hardly making an impression on the huge mattress. Her face was finally relaxed in a sleep of sheer exhaustion, her cheeks still cherry-red from her bout of crying. He sat down on the bed next to her and, reaching out a hand, gently brushed the hair from her brow. She sighed and buried herself even deeper into the mattress. Byron gave an answering sigh and turned off the bedside lamp, casting the room into instant darkness.

*   *   *

Cara woke to find the iron band of Byron's arm around her middle. She stared down at the masculine hairs of his forearm as it lay against her as if it belonged there. It had once belonged there, she reminded herself with a pang of memory that was more pain that simple recollection.

Byron sighed and pulled her closer, as if he sensed her instinct to remove herself from his intimate embrace. She could feel his legs against the backs of her, his rock-hard stomach against the softness of her bottom as he shifted slightly in his sleep.

She wondered when he'd joined her in the big bed. Had he looked down at her with desire burning in his eyes, or had he simply turned back the covers and gone to sleep?

She felt his lips on her shoulder and froze.

'You taste nice,' he said in a deep rumble. 'Like vanilla.'

She didn't dare move. She could already feel the ridged flesh of him against her in response to her nearness.

'Did you sleep?' he asked when she didn't respond.

'Yes.'

'Good.'

She felt him move against her and her stomach gave a sudden lurch.

'What time is it?' she asked, looking for a way out.

'It's early,' he answered, trailing a path of soft kisses down her back.

She shivered in reaction and tried vainly to stop herself from responding.

'Why don't you turn around and say good morning properly?' he suggested.

Cara hesitated.

He kissed her neck as the hand around her waist reached upwards for her breast. Her breath locked in her throat as his palm closed over the mound of her flesh, his fingers searching and finding the hardened nub. She turned in his arms and his mouth found hers, leaving her no time to resist even if she'd been in such a mind to do so. Heat coursed along her veins at the feel of his mouth on hers. His tongue sought entry and she gave it, her mouth opening for him as readily as an orchid to the warmth of the sun after a cold winter.

Her deadened limbs came to life under the expert touch of his hands. Feeling charged throughout her body at the glide of his hands on her flesh. He shaped her breasts as if recommitting them to memory. He explored her mouth as if he'd never discovered it before. He laid her back against the pillows and leaned his rigid length into her softness, reminding her of all the pleasure they'd taken together seven years ago.

Her body was already ready for him. Desire had pooled and prepared her for his invasion, and she could barely think for the need of having him inside her, restaking his claim.

He moved from her mouth, replacing his hands with his lips on her breasts. He'd removed her simple cotton nightie with hands that had trembled against her flesh as if in reverent worship. She sighed as his mouth worked its magic on her, drawing from her a response she had no hope of withholding.

She felt the intimate probe of him and her thighs opened instinctively. He slid into her with a deep groan that sent shivers of reaction up along her spine, filling her emptiness with a completeness she hadn't felt in seven long, achingly lonely years. He set his rhythm and she responded to it as if perfectly programmed to do so. Her breathing increased in pace to match his, her hands shaped him, caressed him just as thoroughly as his did her. Her mouth rediscovered his, her tongue playing with hers in an intimate dance that was mirrored in the movements of their joined bodies. Cara bit down on her bottom lip to stop herself from screaming with the pleasure of his touch.

'Don't hold back,' he murmured near her ear. 'I want to hear you.'

She writhed beneath him and fought against her own response. But finally she had to give in to it. She smothered most of her cry of ecstasy against the breadth of his shoulder, but she felt his smile of satisfaction at her response against her lips as he took her mouth once more.

The sound of his pleasure was a salve to her. It was some sort of compensation to her pride that he was just as affected by her touch as she was by his.

A silence settled between them as they lay still, intimately joined, as if neither of them wanted to be responsible for the first move away.

'I'd forgotten how sensitive you are,' he said after some minutes.

'No doubt you've had plenty of other experiences with which to compare.'

'Perhaps not as many as you think.'

She hated the thought of him with anyone else; it scored her flesh like a barbed weapon.

'What about you?' he asked. 'How many lovers have you had since we parted?'

'Not as many as you'd think.' She used his own words to shield the truth.

He moved away from her and she instantly felt cold without his warmth to fill her.

'I've got to get going.' He reached for his bathrobe. 'I've got a busy day ahead. What about you?'

'I haven't got any consignments, but I thought I'd work on the furnishings for here.'

He reached into the pocket of his jacket, hanging from a chair. He took out a credit card and handed it to her. She took it with a questioning glance.

'You'll need that to organise all the purchases,' he said.

She looked at the card in her hands and felt uncomfortable.

'I can bill everything to my office,' she suggested.

'You can, if you'd rather, but it's still going to be my money that pays for it.'

She didn't have an answer for that, so stayed silent.

'I thought we'd eat out tonight,' he said as he opened the *en suite* bathroom door. 'That is unless you'd prefer to have something simple here and have an early night?'

She didn't have an answer for that either, so simply turned her back and buried herself under the covers. She heard the rumble of his amused laughter and cursed her transparency. She didn't want him to know how much he affected her. It made her feel vulnerable and exposed.

She heard the sound of the shower running and got out of bed, slipping into her bathrobe to make her way downstairs. She ignored the kettle and toaster to go outside and breathe in the fresh morning air as she stood looking out towards the harbour.

The sun was bright but the air felt heavy, as if rain was expected later. The gardens looked fresh and inviting, and she stepped down on to the lush green of the lawn in her bare feet, enjoying the sensation of the cool damp grass between her toes. She lifted her face to the morning sun, closing her eyes to the warmth of its caress on her cheeks.

She heard something behind her and turned around to find Byron standing looking at her.

'Have you got time for a cup of tea?' she asked him, to cover her embarrassment as she brushed past him on her way back to the kitchen.

'No, I'll get something later,' he said. 'I'll call you during the day. Will you be out looking for furnishings?'

She nodded as she searched for teabags. He handed them to her with a small smile.

'Will you be all right?' he asked.

She looked at him blankly.

'Why shouldn't I be all right?' she asked, forcing her features into impassivity.

'Why indeed?' he answered wryly and, scooping up his keys, left the room.

She stared after him and wondered what he'd meant. Was he already regretting what had happened between them this morning? Why should he when he'd been the one to engineer it?

She turned to stir her tea and thought about the intimacy they'd shared. He was probably already choosing names for the baby he was planning for her to conceive. The thought of it made her insides shrink in apprehension. The contraceptive pills she took to regulate her cycle were burning a hole in her toiletries bag—but she wasn't going to stop taking them, no matter what plans he'd made. There was simply no point. He'd surely tire of her after a few months, when she failed to conceive, and she would be cast aside to make room for the next candidate.

The day dragged interminably. Cara wondered if it was because Byron waited at the end of it. Her body tightened in anticipation and a wave of remembered pleasure swept through her, causing her insides to flip-flop in anticipation.

She threw herself into organising the delivery of several rugs from her favourite supplier, as well as buying two large cream leather sofas from the showroom floor. The dining room was easy; she went straight to a large antique warehouse where she purchased an elegant walnut table.

Several lamps and vases later, she was feeling a little more relaxed. She realised with a sudden jolt of surprise that she was actually enjoying herself. Choosing various items for Byron's home had brought a sense of excitement to her usually humdrum day. She told herself it was the experience of shopping with carte blanche that was really responsible for her level of enjoyment, but deep down inside she had a feeling there was far more to it than that.

CHAPTER FIVE

CARA had not long finished dealing with the last delivery of furniture when she heard the sound of Byron's car in the driveway. She dusted off the dining room setting with the soft cloth in her hand and, trying to control the leap of her pulse at the sound of his key in the lock, turned around to face him.

'You've been shopping,' he said, looking around. 'Very nice.'

'It was frightfully expensive.' She screwed up the cloth in her hands and avoided his eyes.

'How expensive?'

She told him and he shrugged.

'I told you to do what you had to do, no price limit. You've done a good job.'

'Thank you,' she said, a rush of warmth filling her at his compliment.

She watched as he stepped down into the lounge room and tested the sofas.

'Come and sit here and tell me what sort of day you've had.' He patted the sofa seat next to him.

Cara tentatively sat beside him, conscious of the way the soft leather gathered around her, drawing her closer towards his strongly muscled thighs.

One of his hands stretched out along the sofa behind her shoulders; the other picked up a stray lock of her hair and gently tucked it behind her ear. The soft brush of his fingers along the sensitive skin of her cheek made her heart squeeze in her chest. How she longed to feel him touch her again!

'So, did you have a good day, Cara?'

She wrenched her eyes away from the movement of his lips as he spoke and concentrated on the black dots on his tie.

'It was OK.'

He tilted her chin with one finger so she had no choice but to look him in the eyes.

'You don't like looking at me, do you?'

She didn't answer; in fact, couldn't answer.

'I want you to look at me,' he said deeply. 'I want to see what's going on behind that cool exterior. I want to see the real Cara, not the cardboard cut-out you usually present to the world.'

She pushed away from his hand and stood up, her expression guarded.

'I need to have a shower,' she said. 'I'm covered in dust from unpacking the furniture.'

He got to his feet, and before she could scoot away he caught her by the wrist and held her fast.

'Don't push me away. I'm trying to help you—can't you see that?'

She glared at his hand around her wrist before lifting her eyes to his.

'You don't want to help me,' she bit out. 'You want to control me.'

'I don't want to control you at all,' he said. 'I want to understand you. Anyone can see how unhappy you are. It positively comes off you in waves.'

'What business is it of yours?' she asked. 'Why didn't you stay out of my life? Why are you suddenly so interested in my emotional state after seven years?'

'Because I made some errors of judgement in the past and I want to make sure I don't make them again.'

She lowered her eyes and swallowed the knot of tension building in her throat.

'I want you to learn to trust me,' he continued. 'To stop seeing me as the enemy and more as your friend.'

'You have a very strange notion of friendship.' Her tone was heavy with sarcasm. 'Friends don't exploit each other; neither do they make impossible demands.'

'Perhaps I should remind you at this point that if I hadn't stepped in, your financial affairs would be in tatters. Your reputation as an interior designer would be shot to pieces—not to mention your partner's.' His voice was edged with steel as he looked down at her.

Resentment burned like a fire in her as she listened to him. She bit her lip to stop herself from flying at him with words she might later have to withdraw. Her anger threatened to spill over, but she clamped down on it with determination. He had her over a barrel and he knew it. She'd seen the figures, and she knew enough about the interior design business to know how quickly the gossip network worked. If word got out they were in trouble, what little business there was would drop off even more.

'I've engaged the services of a business manager,' he said, watching the struggle played out on her face. 'She'll do the books and keep a watchful eye on things.'

'How dare you?' She wrenched herself from his hold and glared at him. 'You've taken over my personal life and, not happy with that, now you've taken over my business as well!'

'Cara, don't let your emotions cloud the issue. Think about it, a business manager will free you and Trevor to spend more time doing the things you're best at.'

'You had no right to go over my head like that.'

'I had every right,' he said, his frustration increasing. 'I've invested a lot of money and I'm not going to sit back and see my efforts go to waste. Besides, what about when you get pregnant? You'll want to cut back on your hours and take things easy.'

'You've got it all planned, haven't you?' Her eyes flashed fire at him. 'What if I don't fall pregnant, according to plan? What then?'

Anger darkened his eyes and his hands reached for her with a renewed strength that she had no hope of circumventing.

'You will get pregnant,' he said in a cold, hard tone. 'I'm going to make absolutely sure of it.'

He pulled her into the wall of his body, his mouth crashing down on hers. Cara tried to escape, but once his lips touched hers she was lost. It was an angry kiss, but she didn't care. His kiss brought her jaded body to instant thrumming life. Her pulse raced at the sensation of his tongue probing for entry and her heart tripped when he achieved it with deft purpose, leaving no part of her mouth untouched.

Her breathing quickened. The hands that had earlier pushed against him to escape were now hanging on to his shirt, her nails digging through the fabric into his chest. She could feel the hard ridge of his erection and her spine loosened in reaction. Her legs quivered as he pushed her down on to the sofa, his hands already under her top, freeing her breasts from her bra. He bent his mouth to each hardened peak, sucking hard as if he wanted to cause her both pleasure and pain. She whimpered as his mouth moved lower, his hands at the waistband of her toffee-coloured trousers.

Suddenly he lifted himself off her and, standing up, scored a pathway through his hair with his hand. His breathing wasn't much steadier than hers she was relieved to see as she struggled upright and tidied the disarray of her clothes.

'I'm sorry.' His tone was gruff. 'I shouldn't have reacted like that. It won't happen again.'

She lifted her chin and, getting to her feet, brushed past him without a word.

'Cara.'

She hesitated on the step out of the lounge, but then thinking better of it continued on as if he hadn't spoken. Byron watched her go, his mouth tightening as he turned to stare at the evening view instead.

'Damn it.' He addressed the harbour in front of him. 'Damn it to hell.'

She came downstairs an hour later, dressed in a brown skirt and a long-sleeved white top, her hair piled on top of her head. Her eyes skilfully avoided his as she asked, 'Do you still want to eat out? I wasn't sure so...' She left the rest of the sentence hanging in the air.

'Yes.'

He reached for his jacket from where he'd thrown it earlier, across the back of one of the stately dining chairs.

'Come on—it's what we both need. Neutral ground.'

She felt inclined to agree with him. The house, large as it was, didn't offer her the same sense of safety a crowded restaurant would.

Some minutes later they were shown to a quiet table in the corner of a small French restaurant, and she had cause to wonder if she'd overrated the safety factor. She didn't feel too safe, sitting alone with him in this private corner, away from the cynosure of the other clientele's eyes.

His eyes met and held hers across the small intimate table.

'There's something I'd like to discuss with you.'

Cara felt her spine stiffen in apprehension.

'Yes?'

He waited until the waiter had placed their drinks before continuing. 'I'm flying to Melbourne the weekend after next. I want you to come with me.'

'Are you asking me or telling me?'

He considered her question for a moment.

'Both. I've already booked the flights. It is an important occasion and I don't want to miss out.'

'Why are you telling me? You've already organised it. What if I don't wish to go?'

'I'd like you to make the effort,' he said. 'My parents are celebrating forty years of marriage. I think it would be nice for us to share in it.'

'It has nothing to do with me. You go; I've got plenty to do to fill my time.'

'My parents would like you to be there.'

She looked at him in consternation.

'You've told them about…about us?'

'Not in so many words. I've told them what they need to know. When they heard we were…' he hesitated over the word '…seeing each other again, they insisted you be invited.'

'We're not "seeing each other", as you so euphemistically describe.' Her tone was cutting. 'You're hoping to use me as a human incubator. Did you tell them that?'

'I don't wish to be drawn into an argument with you, Cara. Certainly not in a busy restaurant. I don't think it's too much to ask to discuss this like two rational adults.'

'I don't want to go.'

He sighed and tried another tack.

'Please, Cara. Fliss would like to see you again. She's missed you over the years. She was devastated when you left.'

Cara thought about his younger sister, picturing her as she had been back then—four years younger than her, full of the vigour of youthfulness, eighteen and on the threshold of adulthood. Even then she had outclassed her school-friends in her academic achievements, with a perfect score in her leaving certificate. Cara imagined her now, with a small child and another on the way, a doctorate already under her belt and still only twenty-five years old. As gifted went, Fliss had certainly upped the benchmark.

'I'll think about it,' she said.

'That's as good as I'm going to get from you, isn't it?'

She inspected his face for bitterness, but instead he was smiling at her wryly. She liked the way his features relaxed when he smiled. She liked the way his dark eyes softened and the way his forehead lost the almost permanent groove she was so used to seeing there whenever he was with her.

'I'm not very good at making promises that far ahead of time,' she confessed reluctantly.

'That's OK,' he said. 'We'll just take it one day at a time. You can tell me in a few days, or if you like even on the Friday morning; the flight doesn't leave until six p.m.'

The waiter came to over them with the daily specials blackboard and Cara was spared the necessity of reply. They ordered their food, and once the waiter had left she felt herself relax a little into the chair, relieved she had a few days before she had to commit herself.

It had been such a busy day, fraught with emotional highs and lows. She wasn't used to dealing with the intensity of an intimate relationship any more. She hadn't ever been that good at it, even when they were married. Byron's expectations of their relationship had been so different from hers.

He came from a secure family background—noisy at times, but totally secure. His parents loved each other, and their four children, and had even made a huge effort to welcome her into the family, though they'd been a little shocked at the speed with which she'd joined it. She suspected they had believed her to be pregnant and desperate for the respectability of marriage, but as the months had gone on their attitude towards her had seemed to improve. It was ironic, really, she thought as she twirled the drinking straw in her glass; they had no sooner begun to accept her when the real trouble between her and Byron had begun.

In truth she'd found the whole exercise claustrophobic. She'd felt as if she couldn't breathe, with everyone so involved in each other's life. She and Byron hadn't spent a single weekend of their short marriage alone. There'd been family picnics or barbecues, or other outings that somehow required each and everyone to attend. Cara hadn't been prepared for such a frenetic lifestyle and had retreated even further into her shell. She'd felt trapped by Byron's desire to start a family and had argued heatedly and repeatedly with him over her use of contraceptives.

She'd left him soon after a particularly vicious row. She still cringed to think of the names they'd thrown at each other. She'd been unwell for weeks, not having picked up properly after a bad bout of flu, and her temper had been frayed beyond the limit by yet another demand for their attendance at a family gathering. Cara had packed her bags and caught the first train to the city, desperate for some breathing space.

Later that day she'd seen Byron in a café with Megan, his childhood sweetheart, the young woman everyone had previously expected him to marry. Megan had obviously been crying and Byron's arm had been around her shaking shoulders, his head bent close to hers. Cara hadn't needed to see any more. Something deep inside her had closed up, as if a door that had been prised apart earlier had finally snapped shut, never to be reopened.

She had caught the next available flight to Sydney and within a week had filed for divorce. She had known he'd come after her, so had covered her tracks until eventually he'd given up. Her lawyer had at one point laid professional interests aside and tried to get her to rethink her actions, but her mind had already been made up. She didn't belong in the Rockcliffe family; she never had. She'd been foolish to think the clash of their backgrounds wouldn't have some sort of effect.

Her mother had gloated over the dissolution of her marriage. Cara hadn't seen her manipulation until it had been too late to escape. The pattern of years had disguised its power over her. It pained her to think of her gullibility, to see the way her mother had so skilfully achieved her own selfish ends, destroying her daughter's life in the process.

Quite by accident Cara had discovered she was pregnant. She had no longer been able to ignore her general malaise, and a routine check-up had uncovered that she was close to six months pregnant. Her mother had been furious. She obviously hadn't wanted Cara to return to Byron and had railed at her to get rid of it, before her life was ruined as hers had been by Cara's birth.

Cara had been in such a low state emotionally that she'd lost concentration whilst driving with her mother to an appointment with a family planning advisor. A car running a red light had slammed into her mother's side of the car. Her mother had been seriously injured, needing months of rehabilitation, and Cara had lost the baby. Her own rehabilitation had been postponed while she dealt with the increasing demands of her mother. She'd been well and truly caught in her mother's trap and there had been no way out.

Every day for the next four years Edna Gillem had berated her daughter for ruining her life, ending her marriage and taking away her every chance at happiness. Cara had been exposed to her mother's vitriol all her life, but somehow her guard had been down further than usual after the loss of her baby. Her mother's hatred had injured her in a place no one had ever been able to reach before. Without even being aware of it she had slipped into the role of her mother's slave, juggling her ever-increasing demands with her own study commitments.

She would never know how she'd got through those years. Somehow she had, but the legacy they had left had marked her for life. She felt damaged. Her mother had spent years trying to destroy her self-esteem and finally she had.

Cara had privately buried the tiny body that hadn't had a chance at life. She'd had her daughter's name engraved on a headstone she'd paid for with money from the divorce settlement. She'd told no one. Her secret was locked away inside, where no one could touch it, but every single time she even heard the name Emma mentioned that secret part of her contracted painfully, reminding her of all she'd lost...

Byron broke into her agonising reverie with a gentle call of her name.

She looked up and stared at him, as if she were surprised to see him sitting opposite her.

'Where did you go?' he asked.

'Go?'

'In your mind. You had that faraway look in your eyes.'

'Did I?'

He reached for her hand, holding it in the warmth of his. 'Tell me, Cara. Don't shut me out.'

She stared at her small cold hand, almost swallowed up by his large one. She thought about telling him, even imagined framing the words in such a way he'd understand, but then decided against it. She still didn't know how he'd heard about her pregnancy. She wanted to find out but didn't want to bring up the subject. It was just too painful, still too raw.

'I was thinking about...about the colour of the rugs for the spare bedrooms,' she lied. 'And curtains. I was thinking about long ruffled pull-back curtains—swathes of fabric that offer privacy without obstructing the view.'

Byron watched the movement of her eyes away from his and knew she was lying. Annoyance flicked along his veins. He wanted to get inside her head, find out everything about her. He'd never met a more complex person in his life and he hated the fact that she made it so clear she didn't need him emotionally.

He decided to let her get away with it this once. Something about the shadowed look in her eyes had alerted him to her fragility, and even though on the outside she presented a cool diffidence he was beginning to see it as a ruse. A very important, significant ruse.

Their food arrived and he watched as she gave every appearance of enjoying her meal, even commenting on the various flavours once or twice.

They left the restaurant in a companionable silence and Byron privately congratulated himself for not pushing her. She reminded him of a flighty horse who balked at the drinking trough. He'd have to think of some other strategy to get her to relax enough to drink.

The house welcomed them with a warmth that secretly delighted Cara. The rugs she'd chosen for the marble floors took away their cold formality and added a cosiness that made the grand house feel more like a home.

Byron poured himself a cognac and sat on the nearest sofa to look over the brochures she'd left on the coffee table. Cara sat opposite, her arms linked around her knees, answering his occasional query over availability.

'I like this.' He pointed to a large gilt edged mirror in one of the antiques brochures. 'What do you think?'

Cara couldn't see it properly, so shifted to sit on the floor at his feet and read the details printed on the bottom. This close, Byron could pick up the sweet fragrance of her hair. She rattled off the details to him, but he wasn't listening. He was imagining her hair splayed out on his pillow, her forehead beaded with the perspiration of spent passion.

'And there's one with a scrolled edge,' she said, turning over the page and pointing to it. 'I saw it the other day. It's rather big, but I think the back wall of the dining room is large enough to carry it. What do you think?'

She swivelled round to glance up at him and her mouth

went dry. He was looking at her intently, as if seeing her for the first time.

'It's…it's more expensive than the other one, but I think it's worth it. I can order it tomorrow and have it delivered and…' She swallowed the rest of her prattle as his hand came out and released the curtain of her hair from its clasp.

He took her hand and she didn't resist as he pulled her to sit beside him on the sofa. Her eyes met his briefly, before fluttering closed as his mouth came down towards hers.

This time his kiss was gentle. He took his time, only increasing the pressure of his lips when he felt her response. He scooped her up in his arms as if she weighed nothing and carried her upstairs to the bedroom, his eyes never once leaving hers.

She explored the depth of his gaze with her own. Words weren't necessary as he laid her on the big bed and reached to loosen his tie. She watched him undress with a steady purpose that secretly excited her. His eyes burned with a heat she could see reflected in his aroused body and her breath hitched in her throat as he came towards her.

He removed her clothes with that same calm intent, laying each article aside as if it were a piece of delicate, fragile lace. His unhurried approach incited her desire as no heady, hasty grasp for fulfillment could do. His eyes caressed every inch of her as he uncovered her, and when she was finally naked he lowered himself and gathered her into his arms.

His mouth took her on a journey of sensuality, leaving no part of her unbranded by his lips or tongue. Her pleasure knew no bounds; her body writhed with contortions of ecstasy, her high, panting cries filling the night air.

He waited until she'd come back to earth before taking his own pleasure. She held him to her, thrilling in the sound of his guttural groan of release, glorying in the collapse of his large body over hers, his ragged breathing filling her ears.

Cara lay in Byron's arms while he drifted off to sleep and thought about the future months. He wanted a child; he didn't want her other than in a physical sense as a means to bringing about that particular goal. But it wasn't going to happen. What place in his life would she have when he finally found out the truth? Would he cut her out of his life altogether?

He'd made it clear he wasn't after a long-term commitment; she couldn't really blame him for feeling that way considering the bitter break up they'd experienced. What man in his right mind would? She knew she was living a lie, but somehow couldn't stop herself. Being in his arms once again was somehow helping her to lay the past to rest. She only hoped he would find it in himself to forgive her when he found out the truth.

She wondered what had happened to Megan. Had he had a brief affair with her and then moved on? Or was she still somewhere waiting in the wings for him?

Cara carefully shifted herself away from Byron's loose hold and, turning to stare at the wall, sighed wearily. Sleep was far away. Her body felt exhausted but her mind was unable to let go of the images that tortured her in her quietest moments. Images of her mother screaming at her—hair wild, eyes drug-glazed—her embittered words like shards of glass tearing at Cara's tender flesh. Words delivered with one purpose and one purpose only—to inflict as much pain as possible.

As a young child Cara remembered being bewildered and frightened by her mother's sudden outbursts, but over time she'd learnt to block them out. She'd taught herself to shut her mind to the rage being played out in front of her, disciplining herself to think of another place or time where she was safe. She'd retreated into herself, imagining herself as someone else, someone who didn't have a dysfunctional mother who loathed the very air she breathed.

After another hour of fighting with the nightmares in her head Cara gave up trying to sleep. She slipped out of the bed, being as careful as she could not to disturb Byron's sleeping form. She slipped on her bathrobe and tiptoed out of the room.

He found her standing at the window in one of the spare bedrooms, the soft glow of moonlight casting a ghostly image over her expressionless face. Her slender figure was without movement. At first he wondered if she were still asleep. He'd heard somewhere that troubled people often walked in their sleep.

'Cara?'

He touched her gently on the shoulder and felt her flinch. He dropped his hand and sighed.

'Can't you sleep?'

She turned to look at him, her eyes dulled, as if they'd just seen something too horrible to comprehend. A trickle of alarm pooled in his stomach but he fought it back to say softly, 'Come back to bed. You look exhausted.'

She looked at him for a few moments, her eyes gradually losing their blank lifelessness. He saw the bright sheen of tears forming and his stomach gave another painful lurch. He held out his arms, and to his surprise she took the one step separating their bodies and stepped into his hold.

He stood looking out of the window across the fragrant cloud of her hair, her head resting just beneath his lowered chin. Her slight body was pressed up against him, as if he were a shelter in a particularly vicious storm. He didn't say a word, just held her and stared at the city in front of him gradually coming to life as the rising sun anointed everything in a warm golden glow.

CHAPTER SIX

THE next week and a half passed far too quickly for Cara. She felt the spectre of the following weekend looming, and knew she'd have to come to a final decision over whether or not to go to Melbourne with Byron.

Over the last few days she'd sensed a subtle change in him. He treated her differently; it was as if he had only just met her and didn't want to do anything that might upset their new relationship. She knew it was because of that night at the window. Something had happened that early morning—something outside of her experience. For the first time in her life she'd felt truly safe. Simply holding her in his strong arms, without saying a word, had salved a raw wound inside her just like a soothing balm.

The rest of the week was spent putting the finishing touches to each of the rooms. The curtains were still in the process of being made, and as soon as one had been completed it was delivered and assembled.

One of the spare bedrooms presented a different sort of challenge. Cara stood in the small children's-sized room, as yet still unfurnished, and wondered what to do. It seemed pointless decorating a room for a child she was never going to have, and yet the thought of preparing it for someone else's child was somehow worse.

Friday morning came, and she still hadn't made up her mind about the Melbourne trip. She watched as Byron shrugged himself into his business shirt and reached for a silk tie.

'I've arranged for the business manager to meet us for

lunch,' he announced. 'I'll pick you up from your office about twelve.'

Cara reluctantly removed herself from the cocoon of the bed and slipped her arms into her bathrobe.

'What about this weekend?' he added, reaching for his shoes. 'Are you planning to come with me?'

She chewed her bottom lip thoughtfully for a moment. He must have sensed her wavering and said encouragingly, 'I'll be there to field any tricky questions over our current arrangement. Just leave it to me.'

Cara felt torn. She didn't want to be swallowed up by the Rockcliffe family, but neither did she wish to spend the weekend by herself. She was getting used to having Byron around. Too used to it.

'I'll come,' she said at last.

'Good girl.' He dropped a swift kiss on top of her head and, snagging his jacket with one finger, added, 'I'll see you at twelve.'

She sighed once he'd left. The house seemed so empty without him there. She was getting far too used to his company, she remonstrated with herself as she stepped into the shower recess in the plush *en suite*. She was becoming dependent. He was beginning to take over her world in more ways than one.

Byron drove towards the eastern suburbs and parked outside a restaurant in Potts Point. Cara followed him to a table inside, where a young woman was already seated, her head bent down over a personal organiser and some papers on the table.

Cara stiffened in shock as the woman lifted her chestnut head to look their way. Megan Fry stood up and, directing her smile towards Byron, lifted her cheek to be kissed. She then turned to Cara, and the smile didn't quite reach her eyes when she held out a perfectly manicured hand.

'Hello, Cara. It's been a long time.'

'Yes,' was all Cara could manage.

They sat down at the table and Megan turned to Byron once more, her china-blue eyes literally dancing with excitement.

'I'm so thrilled to be on board,' she said. 'I've got so many ideas for the business.'

Cara's spine was stiff with resentment and she threw Byron a heated look. He glanced back at her but his expression was unreadable. He turned to Megan.

'Things are in a bit of a mess, Megs. It will take a while to sort out. I think we should take it one step at a time.'

Cara felt herself seething with anger at the thinly veiled insult. She hadn't expected it from him and that made her twice as furious. He'd caught her off guard and it made her feel vulnerable and exposed. She'd begun to trust him and he'd exploited that trust by inveigling his old girlfriend into *her* business.

'What about the other partner?' Megan asked. 'Where's he?'

'He called in sick,' Cara said tightly.

Megan threw Byron an I-bet-that's-a-lie-look and drew his attention to the accounts folder in front of her.

'I've been going through the invoices and I've found there are some outstanding accounts. Should I call the debt collectors in or just send out reminders?'

Cara couldn't believe they were sitting there, with their heads together, discussing her business affairs as if she wasn't there. Anger rose in her like a tide and the palms of her hands began to sting with the pain of having buried her nails into them.

'Reminders this time,' Byron was saying. 'What do you think, Cara?'

'What?' she snapped, frowning at him.

He gave her a long, steady look.

'I asked if you had any preference over how the outstanding debtors are to be approached.'

'No,' she said, lowering her eyes. 'No, I don't.'

'Well...' He swivelled in his chair to address Megan once more. 'That's settled, then. Reminders first round; debt collectors next. Anything else?'

They went on to discuss various aspects of the business, and even though Cara could tell Byron was making an effort to draw her into the discussion at hand she resisted all his attempts and sat in surly silence.

Their food arrived and the conversation switched to other topics. Cara forced herself to listen, although she barely offered a word, even when a question was directed towards her. If Megan thought she was being uncooperative and antagonistic she gave no indication of it. She spent most of the time pressing up against Byron in a manner that demonstrated a long-standing mutual affection. It made Cara sick to her stomach.

After lunch Megan made her way to her own car while Byron escorted Cara back to his. She walked stiffly by his side, but when he put a hand to her elbow to guide her across the street she removed herself from his grasp. She heard him suck in his breath impatiently, his own back rigid with tension as he unlocked the car.

'Must you persist in this childish manner?' he ground out as he wrenched open her door.

She tossed her head in a gesture of defiance and got in the car, her mouth tight. She watched him stride angrily to the driver's side, his own mouth set in a grim line.

'I see how it's going to be this weekend.' He threw her a cold look of disdain. 'Tantrums and the cold shoulder routine.'

'I'm not coming.'

'Yes, you are, goddammit!' He thrust the car into gear with a vicious surge of his hand. 'For once in your life you will do exactly what I say. I don't want my parents' celebration to be spoilt by your petty jealousy—'

'I am not jealous!'

He shook his head and changed lanes.

'You've always had it in for Megan,' he said. 'She's practically family, for God's sake!'

'No doubt she'd like to be,' she muttered under her breath.

'What?'

'Nothing.'

He sighed and took the turn-off towards her office.

'I want your promise, Cara, that you will do your best to conduct yourself in an appropriate manner this weekend. It's very important to me.'

She didn't answer.

'Cara, have I your word?'

She looked out of the window, her shoulders tight with tension.

'Yes.'

They almost missed their flight. By the time they'd both finished work and hurried home to throw some things in a bag, time was slipping away at an alarming rate. The Friday evening traffic didn't ease the tension building in the car, and by the time they finally parked, checked in and boarded the flight Cara had the beginnings of a pounding headache.

She sat silently beside Byron and, ignoring the safety demonstration, buried her head in the in-flight magazine.

They were met in Melbourne by Byron's brother, Patrick. The two men hugged each other unselfconsciously and then Patrick turned to Cara.

It was obvious he was uncertain how to greet her. She could see the indecision on his face as he contemplated kissing her on the cheek or simply shaking her hand. Cara made it easier for him by making the first move. She reached up and kissed his smooth jaw, and then, standing back, gave him a smile.

'Hello, Patrick.'

'Cara.' She saw his throat move up and down in a deep swallow. 'You look marvellous—doesn't she, bro?'

The awkward moment had passed and they made their way out of the airport. Cara felt Byron at her side, and when he reached for her hand she didn't pull away.

The brothers talked non-stop all the way from the airport to the Rockcliffe home at Hawthorn. Cara listened without contributing. She heard about Patrick's twins, Kirstie and Katie, and about his wife Sally recently graduating from art school.

Byron described his new house and insisted his brother bring his family to visit some time soon. There was a warmth about the exchange that secretly impressed her. Growing up as the lonely child of a grossly underfunctioning parent had left her severely short-changed. She hadn't realised the depth of affection that could exist between individual family members, and it was increasingly obvious that Byron's move to Sydney had created somewhat of a gulf in the Rockcliffe family.

'You should see the things Mum's been baking,' Patrick said with a smile. 'She's so excited you both could make it.'

Cara hadn't been overly confident of Byron's mother's welcome, but when the front door opened she was next in line after Byron for an all-encompassing hug. She finally managed to step out of the embrace, her cheeks slightly pink, very conscious of Byron's steady gaze on her.

'Hello, Mrs Rockcliffe.'

'Cara, my dear girl, what's all this nonsense with Mrs Rockcliffe? We've surely moved well beyond that now. Call me Jan. Ah, here's Robert now. Rob, dear—look who's come with Byron after all.'

Cara was swept up into another hug that threatened to crush the life out of her bones, but it brought another tentative smile to her face regardless.

'Mr...Robert,' she greeted Byron's father shyly.

Robert Rockcliffe turned from hugging Cara to slap his eldest son on the back and tease him about who'd won the recent grand final. Byron retaliated by lamenting the unfaithfulness of swinging supporters and the unfair umpire who'd turned the final result. It was all good-natured banter, and Cara felt herself being swept up into it as if she'd never been away.

Patrick's wife Sally came to offer her greetings, as well as the five-year-old twins. Cara felt the breath stall in her throat at seeing the laughing little girls, who were immediately snatched up in a hug by their adoring uncle. Their delighted giggles filled the air and she felt a sensation not unlike pain settle somewhere deep inside.

Over a beautifully prepared roast dinner Cara was seated next to Sally, who'd not long coerced the girls into bed.

'You might think they're adorable,' Sally responded to Cara's shy attempt at conversation. 'But you should have heard the fuss they made about going to bed! Kids.' She shook her pretty blonde head. 'Patrick's keen for another baby, but after twins the first time I'm running scared.'

'I...'

'May I have the salt, darling?'

Cara didn't respond to Byron's request until he touched her on the arm.

'Darling—the salt?'

'Oh.'

She passed it to him, conscious of being the focus of every eye. She wondered if it was obvious to everyone in the room that she hadn't recognised the endearment had been addressed to her.

'This is a fabulous meal, Mum.' Byron took the conversation elsewhere. 'I haven't had a roast since I left.'

Soon after dessert was cleared away the doorbell sounded, announcing the arrival of the rest of the Rockcliffe clan who were calling in for coffee before the real celebrations were to begin the following evening. Cara had cause to wonder if they'd come simply to inspect her, to see if she was worthy of being back with Byron, temporary as it was.

Patrick's twin Leon wasn't as welcoming as his brother had been, but he certainly made an effort to be polite and introduced Cara to his wife Olivia. Their three children were at home with a babysitter, he informed Cara on her polite query about them.

Felicity, Byron's younger sister, squealed with delight when she caught sight of Cara. She threw her arms around her neck as best she could, considering the tight mound of her pregnant belly, and cried in delight, 'You came! How wonderful.'

Cara was swept up by further introductions—firstly to Fliss's husband, a tall, quiet, dark-haired man who seemed a little overcome by the noise and clamour of the combined Rockcliffe clan. Cara wondered if she had at last found an ally. Jason stood to one side as his young wife was enveloped in a hug by her eldest brother, his expression a little bewildered.

Cara made an effort to talk to him over coffee in the spacious lounge room. The rest of the Rockcliffes were arguing profusely over some recent current affair and Jason happened to catch her rolled eyes.

'It takes some getting used to, doesn't it?' He handed her the chocolate truffles.

'Yes.' She smiled tentatively and took one. 'Do you come from a big family?'

He shook his head.

'Only child.'

'Me too.'

Jason cleared his throat and handed her another truffle, which she politely declined.

'Fliss speaks very highly of you,' he said.

'I...I'm flattered,' she answered. 'Please tell me about your son. Byron said he's two. Is that the difficult age everyone makes out?'

It soon became obvious she'd found the right topic to bring Jason out of himself. She spent a very enjoyable ten minutes or so being told everything about his young son. At one point she couldn't stop herself from laughing out loud at one of his dryly delivered anecdotes. The sound of her laughter turned heads, most particularly that of her ex-husband. Cara's laughing smile fell away as she became conscious of the interested gazes turned her way.

Byron came over and, perching himself on the arm of the chair she was sitting in, slipped a casual arm around her shoulders.

'How are things, Jason?' He addressed his brother-in-law. 'Busy in court?'

'You're a lawyer?' Cara asked, and Jason nodded. 'What field do you practise in?'

'Family law,' he answered, just as a silence came over the room. 'Divorce, primarily.'

Cara covered her discomfort with a small smile.

'Interesting work.'

Jan Rockcliffe brandished yet another plate of home-baked treats under Cara's nose as she came bustling past.

'Have one of my ginger balls,' she entreated. 'You too, Jason. Have you lost weight? I shall have to send food parcels to you. Isn't Felicity feeding you properly?'

Cara could almost feel Jason's cringe, but he handled it well, taking one of the proffered delicacies, popping it into his mouth and chewing exaggeratedly. Cara suppressed another giggle and wondered why she hadn't thought of that ploy years ago. It certainly forestalled the need to reply, for Jan Rockcliffe soon gave up and waved the plate elsewhere.

The evening passed in the way most Rockcliffe evenings passed—noisily.

The lively banter of the adult children and their parents interacting, each trying to be heard as the noise level rose, had at first been a culture shock for Cara. She'd forgotten how involved everyone became as various issues were aired. However, there was no sign of anger or opprobrium in the lively exchanges. It was just a big family relating together in the way they had for years.

Cara sat on the fringe and observed Byron's smile as he listened to Fliss tell some joke at Leon's expense. At one point he threw back his head and laughed, and Cara watched as his younger sister's eyes twinkled with mischief. Leon pricked up his ears and, coming over, warned Fliss playfully about picking on someone her own size.

'But I am just about your size,' she laughed, pointing to her protruding stomach. 'Especially now.'

Cara caught Byron's eye on her. He smiled at her and winked one eye, and a trickle of warmth pooled in her belly. She turned away, her colour high, and concentrated on Patrick's story about a work colleague. Robert and Jan sat together on one of the sofas listening, one of Robert's arms slung casually around his wife's shoulders. Cara wondered what had kept them together for forty years. She wondered if they'd ever argued, said things they didn't mean, and whether they'd ever thought about leaving for greener pastures. It certainly didn't look like it, judging from the proud gleam in their eyes as their gazes rested on each of their grown-up children.

Some time later Robert got up with a stretch and announced he and Jan were off to bed. Patrick and Sally exchanged telling glances, suggesting they were thinking the same. They were staying for the weekend, having travelled down from Bright earlier that day, and were tired from the journey after travelling with two lively little girls chattering non-stop all the way.

Leon and Olivia made a move to leave, and Fliss smothered a huge yawn which drew Jason to her side, his hand sliding under the weight of her hair in a gentle caress that spoke of deep, abiding love.

Cara wasn't sure of the sleeping arrangements Byron's mother had organised, and stood to one side awkwardly as the goodbyes were said at the door.

Once the others had left Byron turned to her and held up a bottle of brandy.

'Nightcap?'

She shook her head. 'You have one, though.'

The room seemed very quiet without the lively conversation of earlier. Cara sat on one of the single chairs and looked at a jumble of photographs on the side table at her elbow while Byron sipped his drink.

'You were very quiet,' he observed after an interval of some minutes.

'Was I?' She put the photograph of Patrick and Sally's wedding down and looked at him.

'Very.' He moved across the room to stand in front of her, his hips leaning against the sideboard. 'Everything all right?'

'Of course.'

She toyed with her wristwatch and avoided his eye.

'My mother has separated us,' he announced, bringing her eyes back to his. 'You're in the rose room and I'm in the study.'

'Oh.'

'I didn't enlighten her about our…' He paused for a millisecond. 'Arrangement.'

'I'm sure she'd be very shocked to hear of it,' Cara couldn't stop herself saying.

'No doubt.'

She got to her feet.

'Well, goodnight, then.'

'Goodnight.'

She hesitated, uncertain whether he was expecting her to kiss him. It seemed so cold and clinical to simply leave, considering their intimacy over the past week.

'Cara?'

'Yes?' Her eyes lifted to his once more.

'Come here.'

Two words, a simple command, a temptation too hard to resist. She stepped towards him, her cheeks hot, her palms already moistening.

He looked down at her, his eyes dark, fathomless pools.

'Yes?' It came out as a croak.

He reached out a hand and gently tucked a strand of hair behind her ear, his fingers lingering on the sensitive skin of her neck. She held her breath, her spine liquefying at his touch.

His head lowered and her eyes closed as his lips met hers. It was a gentle, barely there kiss, but it stirred her far more than she'd thought possible. Almost as soon as he'd pressed his mouth to hers he lifted it and stepped away from her.

'Goodnight, Cara. Sleep well.'

She didn't answer. She turned and left the lounge room on legs that were not quite steady.

The rose room had been redecorated since she'd last occupied it, but it still had the same name—even though the walls were now a delicate shade of pearl. Cara peeled back the soft bedlinen, breathing in the fragrant scent of lavender as she tucked herself under the quilted warmth.

She lay listening to the sounds of the big old house sighing, as if in relief that all its family members had come home. The creak of the old staircase as it settled after the last person had traversed it; the old plumbing protesting slightly at being called into service at close to twelve-thirty a.m., and the steady clicking of the grandfather clock in the hall.

Cara counted the minutes, trying to sleep, but her mind wouldn't relax. The lively banter of the evening replayed like a tape in her head, faces flashing in front of her closed eyes: Patrick and Leon with their wives, the adorable twins, Rob and Jan and their forty years of loving, and Fliss with her belly swollen with Jason's second child.

And Byron. His face relaxed as he listened to yet another cute kid's anecdote, showing nothing of his regret at his own childlessness. The way he'd caught her eye occasionally, the slight tilt of his mouth suggesting that, given enough encouragement from her, it would indeed stretch into a genuine smile. The mouth that had met hers in a kiss that had touched her deep inside, as if he were aware of the fragile emotions secretly housed there.

Cara turned into the lavender-scented pillow and wondered if he were already asleep, his large, lean frame taking up most of the sofabed in the study, his long legs hanging over the edge, his arms automatically reaching out to gather her to him even though she wasn't there.

CHAPTER SEVEN

THE house was alive from the very first ray of sunlight. Cara opened her eyes to find herself being observed by two interested identical little faces, their matching pink polka dot pyjamas a perfect foil for their blue eyes and blonde hair.

'Are you our aunty?' one of them asked.

Cara sat up and, brushing the hair off her face, made room for them either side of her on the bed as they clambered up beside her.

'I'm not really sure about that,' she confessed in all honesty. 'I used to be married to your uncle, but I'm not sure if the title still applies.'

The other twin peered at her intently, her blue eyes piercing.

'Why aren't you still married to Uncle Byron?' she asked.

Cara swallowed.

'You don't have to tell us,' the other less forward twin said, glaring at her sister. 'Mummy would say it's none of our business.'

'It is so our business, Kirstie,' Katie said determinedly. 'How else are we to know what to call her?'

'You can call me Cara,' Cara offered. 'That will do for now, won't it?'

Katie gave her a very worldly look.

'Our teacher, Mrs Cuthbert, says children should never call grown-ups by their first name.'

'Oh.'

'But we don't have to tell her,' Kirstie said ingenuously. 'It can be our little secret.'

'Do you like secrets, Cara?' Katie asked, snuggling a little closer.

'I…' Cara opened and closed her mouth.

'I have a secret,' Kirstie whispered conspiratorially.

'Oh?' Cara wasn't sure of the role she should be playing in all of this, so kept a low profile by keeping her input to an absolute minimum.

Kirstie snuggled closer and, cupping her dimpled little hand, breathily relayed her secret to Cara's tingling ear.

'Aunty Fliss is having another baby. I heard Daddy tell Mummy.'

'Oh!'

'I have a better secret than that!' scoffed Katie.

'You do not.'

'I do so. Remember? I told you about it ages ago. When Megan Fry kissed Uncle Byron on his birthday?' She directed her piercing gaze at Cara. 'It was disgusting.'

'Um…'

'She's in love with him,' Kirstie said. 'I heard Granny tell Mummy.'

'I…' Cara looked from one to the other and closed her mouth again.

'I don't like her. She wears too much perfume and pats us on the head all the time. I almost got a headache the last time she came to stay with Granny and Pop,' Katie added in disdain.

Cara could feel her mouth twitching and quickly changed the subject, before she was tempted to pump them for information.

'Do you like stories?' she asked.

Their little faces lit up.

'We love stories.'

'Well.' Cara settled her arms around each young shoulder and began. 'Once upon a time there was a little girl who was very lonely. She didn't have any brothers or sisters, and her father had left long before she'd been born. Her mother was lonely too. So lonely that she didn't really take much notice of her little girl, other than to feed her and growl at her whenever she did something wrong. But one day the mother didn't growl at her little girl; she shouted instead. The little girl didn't understand the reason why her mother was so angry at her, and tried to be extra good to avoid it happening again...'

Cara was lost in the story and hadn't noticed the door of the rose room open slightly. Byron stood watching the scene before him silently. His two little nieces were snuggled up on either side of Cara, their faces trained on her, their eyes wide with captivation.

Cara heard a movement at the door and looked up, her story suspended at the sight of Byron standing there, his expression indecipherable. The twins tugged at both of her arms.

'Don't stop!' Katie implored.

'What happened next?' Kirstie's eyes were bug-like.

Cara smiled regretfully at them both.

'To be continued...'

'Oh, no!' Katie wailed theatrically. 'I hate "to be continued" stories.'

'When will you tell us some more?' Kirstie asked. 'Tonight? When we go to bed?'

She was cornered and both the girls knew it—she could tell.

'All right, then,' she said. 'I'll tell you the rest tonight.'

The girls turned to their uncle.

'Aunty Cara's telling us a story that's a...a...equal...' Kirstie hunted vainly for the correct term.

'Sequel,' Katie said authoritatively.

'Can I listen in too, tonight?' Byron asked, his eyes sliding to Cara's.

'No,' Katie said adamantly. 'This is girls' stuff—isn't it, Aunty Cara?'

Cara was still recovering from being addressed as aunty, not once but twice.

'I'm not sure—'

'Girls only—sorry, Uncle Byron.' Katie grinned up at him cheekily.

'You minx,' he growled, and tickled her playfully.

Not to be left out, Kirstie lunged at him and tickled him in defence of her sister. Cara couldn't help squealing when a stray tickle caught her under the ribs.

'You…' she gasped as she poked her fingers into Byron's rock-hard stomach.

The twins were giggling uncontrollably at the glint of mischief in their uncle's eye as he made another lunge at Cara.

'Oh!' Cara gasped again. 'Stop! Please!'

Her legs were tangled in the sheets so escape was impossible. His face was close, his eyes glittering with some indefinable emotion. Cara felt her breath catch as he addressed the goggle-eyed little girls over his shoulder:

'Katie and Kirstie, Granny's got your breakfast ready downstairs. Why don't you go down and get started while I teach Aunty Cara the rules about tickling?'

The girls scampered off, their laughter ringing down the hall as they went in search of their grandmother.

He turned back to Cara, locked between his forearms on either side of her waist. She met his dark gaze, her stomach tilting at the glitter of naked desire reflected there.

'So,' she said in an attempt at lightening the atmosphere, 'what exactly are the rules of tickling?'

She watched as his mouth stretched into a smile and her stomach gave another lurch.

'The golden rule is, don't do it if you can't take it yourself.' His voice was deep and silky. 'Can you take it, Cara?'

'I...' She swallowed as his mouth came closer. 'I think so...'

'Let's see, shall we?'

His mouth closed over hers and she felt herself sink into the mattress on a sigh of pleasure at the caress of his lips. He deepened the kiss, sending her even further back into the mattress. Her legs opened to make room for him as he stretched over her. She could feel his hard length so close it was a torment to have both the barrier of clothes and the bedlinen that still encased her trembling legs.

He slid one warm hand under her silky pyjama top, his fingers sliding over the aroused peak of one breast until she thought she would cry out with the sensation. He removed his hand and lowered his head, taking her nipple into the cavern of his hot mouth, rolling his tongue over the tight bud, grazing her tender flesh with his teeth. She writhed under his ministrations, her breathing hard, as if she'd just run a race. He left her breasts briefly to return to her mouth, his tongue taking hers on a dance of probe and retreat until all thought was driven from her mind.

She could only think of his body pressing hers to the mattress, his pulsing arousal almost burning through the fabric that separated her soft flesh from him. She could feel him poised, ready and eager to take her to the heights of fulfilment. She could sense the urgency of his need as he explored her mouth. She could feel her own response in secret, preparing her for the slide of his rigid form that would completely fill her aching emptiness.

There was the sound of voices just outside the door and Byron lifted himself from her, his expression rueful as he dragged a hand through his dark hair.

'I'll finish this later,' he promised as he stood up. 'I'll see you downstairs—I think that's the breakfast cue.'

Cara could hear the sound of voices as the family gathered downstairs in the big kitchen. She heard Patrick ask his father if the paper had been delivered, and she heard Sally implore Katie to wash her hands after touching the cat. Sounds of the house coming to life filled her ears, but all she could think about was his promise. He was going to finish what he'd started later.

After a quick shower, she came downstairs. Byron's mother handed her a bowl and directed her towards the breakfast buffet she'd laid out on the sideboard.

The kitchen table was surrounded by the rest of the family in the process of eating breakfast, and she murmured a shy greeting.

'Mummy, Aunty Cara is telling us a story,' Katie said with her mouth full of scrambled eggs.

'Don't speak with your mouth full, darling,' Sally said before adding, 'That's nice of her. What's it about?'

'It's about a little girl who doesn't have anyone to love her,' Kirstie put in.

'How sad.' Sally flicked a brief glance towards Cara before turning back to her daughters. 'Does it have a happy ending?'

'We don't know,' Katie said dramatically. 'It's to be continued.'

'I love happy endings,' Kirstie said dreamily. 'Does she get to kiss a handsome prince in the end?' she asked Cara, her chin on her hands.

Cara smiled wistfully. 'Yes, she does.'

'Yuk!' Katie said, screwing up her face. 'I hope it's not one of those kisses like Megan and Uncle Byron had.'

'*Katie!*' Her mother's face was bright pink as she scolded her daughter.

'It's all right, Mummy,' Katie reassured her guilelessly. 'I've already told Aunty Cara about it.'

The silence was deafening.

Cara bent her head to her plate and pretended to be interested in the food still sitting there untouched.

'Girls—' Sally's voice was tight '—please finish your breakfast. Pop said he'd take you to the Victoria market while I help Granny with the party preparations.'

The little girls jumped down from the table and took their grandfather's hands, following him out of the room chattering animatedly as they went.

'Cara, I'm sorry—the girls can be precocious at times.'

'Please don't worry.' Cara smiled at Sally hesitantly. 'It's fine—really.'

She felt Byron's hooded gaze on her and made another attempt at her muesli.

'Byron, dear.' His mother handed him a plate of bacon. 'Have some more. You too, Cara. You don't seem to be enjoying that muesli. What about some eggs and bacon instead?'

She shook her head, not trusting herself to speak. It seemed like every eye was trained on her, trying to gauge her reaction to Katie's bombshell.

Byron took the plate and helped himself to a portion before handing it back. He turned to glance at Cara.

'I've got a few things to do in town this morning,' he said. 'Do you want to come with me? You could have a wander around the shops and galleries if you like.'

'I…' She put down her spoon and glanced uncertainly at Byron's mother. 'Perhaps I should stay and help your mother and Sally with the party?'

'No.' Jan scooped up the discarded plates. 'You go and explore the shops. Sally and I have got this covered. Mrs Timsby is coming at eleven to help as well.'

'If you're sure?' Cara glanced between Sally and Jan Rockcliffe.

'Go.' Jan waved a teatowel at them both. 'It will do you good. Catch up on old times, or whatever it is divorced couples do these days.'

Cara's face felt hot.

'Come on.' Byron got to his feet. 'Let's go.'

She waited until they were in the car, out of earshot of the house, before she spoke.

'What did your mother mean by that?'

'By what?' He looked at her briefly before checking for traffic as he backed out.

'Her comment about "whatever it is divorced couples do". What did she mean?'

'Who knows?' He shrugged.

Cara chewed one of her nails.

'Perhaps she saw us,' she said.

'Doing what?'

'You know. Kissing in the bedroom. I thought I heard someone go past the door.'

'I wouldn't worry about it if I were you,' he reassured her. 'I'm sure my mother can handle it.'

'No doubt she's got used to you kissing all sorts of women,' she put in, pleased at how nonchalant she sounded.

She felt his glance rest on her.

'Megan and I are just friends.'

'I see.'

'No, you don't see.' His voice hardened. 'You want to make me feel guilty for daring to replace you, don't you?'

'And did you?'

'Did I what?'

'Replace me.'

There was a taut silence.

'If you're asking have there been other women—yes, there have.'

Cara's chest felt tight, as if someone had thumped her, winding her so badly that every subsequent breath she took hurt.

'What about while we were married?' she asked through stiff lips. 'Were there other women then?'

He gave her an incredulous look before turning back to face the traffic.

'I can't believe you just asked that,' he said heavily.

'Why? Because you thought I didn't know?'

'No, because I can't believe you would be so stupid as to throw away our marriage on petty suspicion. I take it you're referring to Megan?'

'I saw you with her,' she said in a cold, hard tone. 'The day I left.'

'And?'

Cara flicked her eyes his way, noting his white-knuckled grip on the steering wheel.

'You were up close and personal.'

'So?'

'So I decided to leave and give you both some room.'

'Cara, I'm finding this hard to take in. Are you saying you left me because you thought I was having some sort of clandestine affair with Megan Fry?'

'It wasn't the only reason I left. I was tired of the fights, the way your family demanded so much of you all the time. We never had a weekend to ourselves in the whole time we were married.'

'We weren't married all that long,' he pointed out wryly.

'We didn't even have a proper honeymoon,' she continued bitterly. 'You were so absorbed in your work you didn't even see what was happening.'

'Cara, running a business takes time and effort. I'd just got the thing up and running when we met. I couldn't abandon ship just then to go off on an extended holiday. I told you that at the time and you seemed to accept it.'

'Your parents wanted you to marry Megan, not me. I knew it from the very first day.'

'Oh, for God's sake! You're making them sound like tyrants. They've only ever wanted what was best for me. They'd never dream of coming between us like that.'

'You surely don't deny that everyone expected you and Megan to get together?'

'No, I don't deny it. But it didn't happen. I married you.'

'Unfortunately.'

'As it turned out. But at the time I thought I was doing the right thing,' he said. 'We both made mistakes. It was a long time ago and we've both moved on—surely?'

Cara didn't answer. She hadn't moved on. That was the trouble. She couldn't. She felt stuck, as if her life had been on pause since she'd left him seven years ago.

'I'll be about two hours,' he said into the silence. 'I'll drop you off near the mall. I'll meet you at one on the corner near the tram stop.'

Cara got out of the car when he pulled into the kerb. She watched as he drove on, deftly manoeuvring his mother's BMW back into the flow of traffic. Once he'd disappeared from sight she turned and sighed.

The mall was bustling with people and trams. Buskers were littered about, their various genres of music filling the air with a cacophony of sound. Several people with promotional brochures approached her, but she ignored them.

She headed towards the larger department stores, taking her time wandering through the floors, stopping to look at various things along the way. She wanted to buy a gift for Byron's parents and after an hour found it. It was a glass dome with a perfect dandelion puff encased inside, where it was totally safe; no wind or breath could disturb the tiny seed formation. She turned it over in her hands and smiled wistfully. It was perfect.

Byron was waiting for her when she got to the corner. He was on foot, having left the car at his office. He eyed the package in her hand as she joined him.

'Is that all you could manage in two hours?'

She nodded.

'I wanted to buy your parents a gift.'

He looked surprised.

'I'm sure they don't expect—'

'I wanted to.'

He took her arm and led her away from the milling crowds to a quiet coffee shop in a nearby arcade. Once they were seated he looked at her across the table, his expression suddenly serious.

'Cara, I think we need to talk about—'

'Byron! Fancy meeting you here.' A female voice spoke from just behind Cara.

'Hello, Sandra.' Byron's greeting wasn't enthusiastic. 'Cara, this is Sandra. Sandra, this is Cara.'

Cara turned in her seat to offer a hand, but Sandra was looking at Byron, seemingly ignoring her presence. She dropped her hand and sat watching the interaction between her ex-husband and the other woman.

'Megan tells me you've offered her a job,' Sandra said. 'Some run-down business that needs picking up?'

Cara stiffened.

'Yes, I have offered her a position,' he said, avoiding Cara's heated glare to face Sandra. 'What are you up to these days?'

'Oh, this and that,' she said with a flirty little smile. 'You didn't call before you left for Sydney.' Her full mouth pouted. 'Did you lose my number?'

Byron looked uncomfortable.

'No, I've been busy.'

'Oh, well.' Sandra tilted one voluptuous hip. 'You know where I am when you need me.'

Cara didn't care for the sound of that little statement. Jealousy ripped through her as she watched the other woman run a finger down Byron's forearm in a suggestive manner.

Byron shifted slightly and Sandra's hand fell away. She turned to look at the silently fuming Cara, her eyes running over her assessingly.

'So, do you work for Byron too?'

'In a fashion,' Cara answered coldly.

Sandra seemed satisfied with that, and after a few more desultory words went on her way.

'Sorry about that,' Byron said once she'd gone.

Cara lifted one finely arched brow.

'Another one of the replacements?'

He rolled his eyes and picked up the menu in front of him.

'If you don't mind, I'd like to change the subject. Sandra Hollingsworth was one of the biggest mistakes of my life.'

'Even bigger than me?'

He put the menu back down.

'You weren't a mistake,' he said.

'What was I?'

He gave her question considerable thought.

'You were the best and the worst thing ever to happen to me.'

Cara's mouth twisted ruefully.

'I suppose I asked for that.'

He smiled lopsidedly.

'You did, didn't you?'

The conversation moved on to other topics, to Cara's immense relief. She found the thought of Byron with any other woman a total anathema to her. She hated to think of him in the throes of passion with anyone else. She hated to think of him kissing another mouth, caressing someone else, loving someone else. It didn't seem fair when she still loved him after all this time.

She stared at the menu in her hands, the words blurring. She still loved him. It was as clear to her as if it were written on the menu in front of her. She loved Byron Rockcliffe and had never ceased doing so.

'Cara?'

She put the menu down and looked across at him. He

indicated the hovering waitress and she rattled off an order she knew she wouldn't be able to force past the huge lump in her throat.

She loved him. She still loved him.

The waitress left with their orders and Byron sat back in his chair, surveying her troubled expression.

'What's going on in that head of yours?' he asked.

Cara blinked at him.

'Sorry?'

'I said, I wonder what's going on inside your head.'

'Nothing much,' she answered. 'I was thinking of your nieces. They're cute, aren't they?'

'Very,' he said. 'I didn't realise you had such magnetism where children are concerned. I thought you hated kids.'

'I don't hate kids,' she said. 'I just choose not to have them. I quite like other people's.'

'And they have certainly taken a shine to you.'

'Yes, well, I didn't have much choice. They came in and started telling me things I didn't want to know. I tried to distract them with a story but you interrupted it.'

'Why didn't you continue?' he asked. 'I wouldn't have stopped you.'

She gave him an ironic glance.

'I'm sure you know how the rest of it goes—although I'll have to give the girls a sanitised version. I can't have their innocence shattered by having the prince and princess getting divorced.'

She sneaked a look at his face, but he was frowning as if deep in thought.

The waitress came with their order and Cara did her best to rearrange the food on her plate in a semblance of eating. She looked at Byron once or twice and he seemed to be doing exactly the same thing. The foccacia melt shifted position several times without actually making it to his mouth.

After a few minutes he pushed the plate aside.

'Cara?'

She looked across the table at him, her expression guarded.

'Yes?'

'I want you to tell me about your mother,' he said. 'Not just her name, not just her occupation, but everything. I want to know what she did to you to make you so unhappy. I think I have a right to know.'

Cara pushed her own plate away and avoided his eyes.

'She's dead. That's all you need to know.'

'No, damn it, it's not.' His tone was impatient. 'The more I think about it, the more I get the feeling you're hiding something—something important.'

'I don't want to talk about this,' she hissed at him, conscious of the other diners seated around them.

'Was she abusive?'

Cara's hands tightened in her lap.

'Did she hit you?'

She got to her feet and left him sitting at the table surrounded by their untouched food.

He joined her in the mall a minute later, after he'd thrown some money at the cashier.

'Cara, I realise how difficult this must be for you, but—'

'You know nothing of what I feel. Nothing.' Her voice was cold and unemotional.

'So tell me.'

'I can't.'

'Why not?'

'Because I…' She looked away into the crowds, her eyes becoming distant.

'Tell me, Cara.'

She turned and faced him, her expression blank, her voice devoid of all feeling.

'I spent twenty-two years of my life pretending I had a mother who loved me. I spent another four years after our divorce coming to terms with the fact that she had never done so. My mother hated me. I have to live with that every day of my life. Please don't ask me to talk about something which causes me so much distress.'

She heard him sigh, felt his warm hand reach for hers, felt his fingers squeeze her hand briefly.

'Come on, honey.' He tucked her arm through his. 'Confession time over. Let's go shopping.'

Cara fell into step beside him, her brow furrowing slightly. His casual endearment tortured her in its poignancy. He'd been the first person ever to call her that, and even though she knew he no longer loved her it comforted her a little to think he'd allowed his resentment to fade just enough to address her in such a manner now.

CHAPTER EIGHT

'How about this?' Byron held up a sheath of silk georgette. 'You'd look sensational in this.'

'It's nice.' Cara fingered the silky green and silver fabric and wondered how she'd allowed him to talk her into this. They'd spent the last hour touring the designer boutiques, stopping occasionally for her to try something on so Byron could give his verdict.

She tried on the green and silver dress and twirled in front of him for his inspection. She hoisted up the hem and stood on tiptoe as she eyed her reflection in the full-length mirror.

'I need higher shoes,' she said. 'What do you think?'

His eyes burned as he ran them over her. She felt her skin prickle. It was as if he touched her all over, his warm hands cupping her flesh, stroking her in places no one but him had touched her before.

'I think that dress should come with a warning.' His tone was wry.

She tilted her head questioningly and he smiled.

'Wearer beware. Men are likely to act with uncontrollable lust when this dress is worn by a petite brunette with golden highlights.'

She turned back to the changing room without responding, but a tiny smile tugged at her mouth and there was nothing she could do to stop it.

She came out to find him with the dress in a designer bag, which he handed to her. She took it hesitantly, her eyes meeting his as he smiled down at her.

'Now for the shoes.'

He insisted on paying, and bustling her in and out of

shops like a whirlwind, coaxing her into choosing lacy underwear, sampling heady perfumes and hunting down the perfect pair of shoes for her new dress. She worried about the amount. Every time she protested about the expense of an item he held up to her he'd roll his eyes and take it straight to the cashier. She soon learnt to keep her mouth shut, and secretly she was pleased. She knew he was trying in a roundabout way to apologise for pressing her about details of her childhood, but it didn't take away from the enjoyment of indulging herself at his expense—especially when he smiled at her encouragingly as she showcased yet another outfit.

As far as retail therapy went, Cara was sold. She hadn't realised how distracting spending money could be. The fact that it was Byron's money and not hers didn't totally dampen her pleasure in being spoilt, however it made her feel slightly uneasy all the same. She felt like a cheat. She wasn't playing by his rules at all, and the thought of him finding out secretly shamed her.

Byron was eventually satisfied with the purchases they'd made and ushered her back to his car, carrying the numerous bags for her as she fell into step beside him.

'How many guests are coming this evening?' she asked conversationally as they headed back towards Hawthorn.

'About fifty or so,' he answered. 'Friends of the family, a few relatives and so on. I'm sure you'll find someone other than me to talk to.'

She flicked him a quick glance.

'I don't mind talking to you,' she said.

'Don't you?' His tone sounded surprised. 'Then why seven years without a word?'

She stared at her hands tightening in her lap before answering.

'I needed some space—'

'Space?' He thrust the car into gear as the lights changed

ahead. 'We could have sorted it out. You didn't give us a chance. You just hightailed it out of my life and left me to face all the questions.' He gave the gearstick another thrust and added, 'Do you have any idea what it was like for me? My family were on my back the whole time, prying for information. Had I upset you? Had I neglected you? God, I was nearly mad with my own feelings, let alone theirs.'

Cara listened to his embittered words with shock. She hadn't until this moment truly thought about what he might have had to go through. She'd simply imagined he'd be relieved she'd left so he could pick up where he'd left off with Megan.

'Look.' His voice had softened somewhat. 'I'm beginning to realise you've had it pretty rough as a kid, and knowing that I'm prepared to make allowances. But at some point you have to realise you can't be a victim all your life. In a way, clinging to the victim role is a little selfish. It doesn't change the past one iota—all it does is stuff up the future.'

'So this plan of yours for me is one of reform?' Her tone was tight with scorn. 'You think by forcing me to live with you will somehow reset the imbalance?'

His hands tightened on the wheel as the next set of lights turned to red, his jaw clenched, his mouth set in lines of frustration.

'I want us to put the past aside and concentrate on the future. Is that so much to ask?'

'I didn't belong in your life before,' she said in a cold, detached tone. 'I sure as hell don't belong in your future.'

'Why?' His dark eyes flashed to hers. 'You live like a bloody nun, shut up in that ivory tower you've so carefully constructed, with "poor me" painted all over the sides. Wake up, Cara. You're a young woman with your whole life ahead of you. Take it by both hands and live, for God's sake.'

'I suppose this morning's shopping spree was meant to entice me, was it?'

'No, of course not. I just wanted—'

'I will not be bought.' Her tight voice cut him off, conveying the anger brewing in her. 'It would take more than a few designer dresses and lacy underwear to sway me. Much more.'

'What would it take?'

Cara's eyes clouded with confusion.

'What would it take for you to come to me willingly?' he asked again, when she didn't answer. 'To live with me as my wife once more? To raise a family together, to build a life together?'

'It would take a miracle.'

He parked the car behind his father's Mercedes and looked across at her.

'What sort of miracle?'

She couldn't quite hold his gaze, and concentrated on the black button of the glove compartment until it started to blur before her.

'It would take love. Something we both no longer have.'

There was a long silence.

'We had love once and it didn't hold us together. Maybe what we need this time is commitment. Lots of marriages are very successful only because the couple are truly committed to the task of bringing up a family,' he said.

'Wouldn't it be better to have both love and commitment?' she asked.

She heard him sigh.

'Life doesn't always go according to plan, Cara. Sometimes one has to work with what one's got and take it from there.'

She followed him into the house, her heart heavy. He didn't love her. She'd destroyed that love by leaving seven years ago. Now he was prepared to settle for second best.

But could she commit herself to a lifetime of sterile politeness? What about passion and heart-tripping desire? She knew he desired her. He'd proved that unreservedly. But he was a man with needs and those needs were perfectly natural, it really had nothing to do with her personally. He'd already informed her there had been other women. It hurt to think of him with someone else. It was like a pain that wouldn't go away.

The Rockcliffe house was buzzing with activity. The helium balloons had arrived and were being positioned in strategic places. The florist had not long left, after delivering huge arrangements of fragrant blooms which Sally was busily placing about the house. She was bustling past the foyer as Cara and Byron entered the house, and smiled at them over the top of an artistic array of white lilies and gypsophila.

'Been shopping?' She eyed the designer bags in her brother's hands. 'Gosh, Cara. Don't tell me you got him to go shopping with you? How did you do it? Patrick positively loathes it.'

'I—'

'We packed in a hurry.' Byron came to her rescue. 'She didn't have anything to wear.'

Sally gave them both an engaging grin.

'It's a good line, that. I should use it more often.' She put the floral arrangement down on the hall table before adding, 'Oh, I nearly forgot. Megan's coming after all. She managed to get a standby flight. Can you pick her up from the airport at five?'

Cara felt the slide of Byron's glance towards her, but she made a show of sniffing at the arrangement Sally had just set down.

'Sure. Which airline?'

Cara didn't listen. She turned towards the kitchen, where there was the aroma of savoury food being prepared, and hoped there was a job she could volunteer for that would effectively remove her from her ex-husband's presence for the rest of the afternoon.

Jan Rockcliffe was agonising over the mini-quiches when Cara walked in.

'Oh, hello, Cara.' She looked up from the tray of pastry cups she was pressing into the tin. 'I think I've made too many salmon ones. What do you think?'

Cara was glad of the distraction and happily involved herself in chopping bacon and sprinkling grated cheese into the rest of the pastry cases, ready for the beaten eggs. Jan chatted to her casually as they worked.

Cara could tell she was taking extra care to keep the conversation on neutral topics. They seemed to discuss just about everything, but there was one thing Cara knew Jan wanted to speak of most—the one thing Cara most dreaded. Neither of them mentioned Byron or the divorce. Jan asked her about her work, and about her mother, but Cara neatly deflected the conversation back to the party preparations.

'I think these ones are just about done.' She placed a tray of perfectly cooked baby quiche on the cooling rack on the large workbench for Jan's inspection.

'Mmm.' Jan prodded at one with an experienced finger. 'Good. Now, how about a cup of tea? Rob should be back with the girls shortly. Best we have a cup in peace, before they come in and take over the kitchen.'

'They're lovely children,' Cara found herself saying as she wiped her hands on a teatowel.

Jan gave her an indulgent look.

'I adore all my grandchildren. You'll meet the rest of them tonight. I wouldn't hear of them not being here to celebrate with us, although I know what their parents would've preferred. I might be celebrating forty years of marriage, but I'm still young enough to remember what it was like to have four young children running underfoot.'

Cara perched on one of the kitchen stools as Byron's mother filled the kettle. Jan switched it on and turned back to face her, the soft lines of her face relaxing into friendliness instead of the distant formality that had lingered there earlier.

'I didn't really want to have children,' she confessed, and Cara straightened in surprise. 'But things weren't as they are now and pregnancy was hard to avoid.'

Cara couldn't think of a single thing to say.

'But when I lost our first baby I was so upset I couldn't wait to fall pregnant again. We women are funny, contrary creatures, don't you think?'

It was hard for Cara to hold the older woman's gaze. She took the cup of tea Jan passed her and cupped her fingers around its warmth.

'Byron didn't tell me you'd…lost a baby. I'm so sorry.'

Jan's smile was touched with remembered sadness as she stirred sugar into her own cup of tea.

'It was a long time ago. A stillborn child wasn't considered a serious loss. Not like now, when you get to hold the infant and say a proper goodbye.'

Cara abandoned her tea.

'How…how far along were you?'

Jan's chocolate-brown eyes, so like her son's, clouded briefly and Cara wished she hadn't asked such a personal and painful question.

'Six months.'

Cara could feel tears prickling at the back of her own eyes as she faced the pain in those of her ex-mother-in-law.

'It was a little girl,' Jan said, even as the question was forming on Cara's tongue. 'She would be thirty-eight by now.'

'I'm so sorry.'

Jan picked up her tea once more. Cara watched as she stirred it unnecessarily for a long moment before speaking.

'Grief is a strange thing, Cara,' she said at last. 'It's like a cardigan in your wardrobe you really should give away but you just can't. You need it to be there, somewhere at the back, just to remind you. You take it out occasionally to look at it, and you always put it back just out of sight, but you know it's still there. Do you know what I mean?'

Cara swallowed deeply and nodded, not trusting herself to speak.

'Thirty-eight years is a very long time, I know, but we each have to deal with things in our own way,' Jan said reflectively.

They sipped their tea in silence. Cara could hear the sound of voices in the background—excited voices getting ready for a party. She lifted her gaze back to Byron's mother and before she could stop herself asked, 'Did you name her?'

Jan put her cup down right in the middle of her saucer with a precision Cara secretly envied. Her own hands were shaking as she placed them in her lap.

'Not for a long time,' Jan answered quietly. 'It wasn't encouraged. But one day some weeks later I decided she deserved a name, and so I called her Anne. Anne Elizabeth Sarah Rockcliffe.'

Cara wanted to tell Byron's mother of her own loss, but just then there was the sound of childish excitement and the twins burst into the kitchen, waving plastic carrier bags in front of them.

'Look what Pop bought me!' Katie crowed excitedly.

'I want to show Granny first.' Kirstie pushed past her sister. 'You always get to show her first.'

'Show me,' Cara said, quickly defusing the situation.

Both the girls came to her, and she made all the right noises over the trinkets Byron's father had purchased. She escorted the twins out of the kitchen with a promise to do their hair for the party, adorning it with the colourful slides their grandfather had bought at the market for them. Sally gave her a grateful glance as she passed them in the doorway, a tray of champagne glasses in her hands.

'You're an angel, Cara,' she said. 'Byron's just left for the airport, and Fliss and Jason just called to say they're on their way. The girls know which dresses they're wearing, but if you could help them that would be great.'

'No trouble,' Cara said, shepherding the twins in front of her up the stairs. 'Come on, girls.' She addressed the children on either side of her. 'Let's get ready to party.'

The guests started arriving at six, and Cara hardly had time to do her own make-up, so busy was she with the twins. She was conscious that somewhere amongst the gathering downstairs Megan Fry would be ingratiating herself into the family fold as if she'd never been out of it. The thought of the other woman telling everyone what a mess Cara's business was in made anger coil in her belly like a snake.

'Can I have some lipstick, too?' Katie asked as she watched Cara apply a subtle rose to her lips.

Cara forced her fingers to relax enough to paint the tiny upturned mouth with delicate precision.

'What about this?' Kirstie held up a palette of eyeshadow in browns and pinks. 'Can I wear some?'

Cara bent down and gently brushed some shadow on each tiny eyelid, hoping Sally wouldn't mind her little girls playing at grown-ups. She was just putting the finishing touches to Kirstie's shuttered eyes when she heard Katie swing around to greet her uncle.

'Uncle Byron! Do you think I look beautiful?'

Cara straightened in time to catch the heart-stopping smile on his face.

'You both look scrumptious,' he said, winking at them.

'What about Aunty Cara?' Kirstie asked. 'Does she look scrumptious too?'

Cara could feel the warmth of his gaze as it ran over her assessingly. In the soft light of the bedroom her silvery green dress shimmered, its silky folds clinging to her lovingly, highlighting the slimness of her body yet enhancing the thrust of her breasts where the fabric dipped to reveal the shadowed cleft between them. Her hair was curling around her face, two or three blonde highlights falling across one cheek, giving her a sultry, seductive look.

Their eyes met and held across the top of the twins, who were looking up at each of them like spectators at a tennis match.

'She looks gorgeous,' he said simply, his eyes burning into hers.

Cara felt her breath catch somewhere between her chest and throat at the intensity in his look. She felt certain that if there weren't two very interested little faces watching them he might have acted right then and there on the message being reflected in the dark depths of his heated gaze.

'What about perfume?' Katie broke the silence that had fallen between them. She began rummaging in Cara's toiletries bag before Cara could tear her eyes away from Byron's. Cara vaguely registered the sound of her cosmetics being sorted, but still Byron's gaze held hers.

'What are these tablets for?'

Cara stiffened in cold fear. She turned to see Katie holding up her packet of contraceptive pills, a questioning look on her young face.

'I...'

Cara felt the weight of Byron's look and her mouth dried up completely. The silence was brief, but it spoke volumes. Byron reached out a hand for the packet.

'Give them to me, sweetheart.' He straightened and, tapping both girls on the tip of their noses, sent them on their way. 'You two run along and show Mummy how nice you look. Uncle Leon and Aunty Olivia will be here soon, and I think Aunty Fliss and Uncle Jason have just arrived.'

The girls scampered off excitedly. Cara stood frozen to the spot, her palms damp with fear as she watched Byron silently examine the packet in his hands.

It seemed a long time before he handed them back to her. Her hand trembled slightly as she took the packet and placed it back in her toiletries bag. A thousand words came and went in her head, but not one came out of her mouth.

Her eyes came back to his hesitantly.

'You need more time, don't you?' he said.

She blinked up at him in disorientation. It wasn't what she'd expected him to say. She'd expected him to lambast her with accusations of cheating on the deal, of tricking him into rescuing her business for nothing.

She tried to hide her inner confusion from his probing eyes. There was no way she could tell him the truth—the painful, irreversible truth.

He sighed and with one hand disturbed the neat arrangement of his dark hair as he moved away from her. She watched him as he picked up the hairbrush she'd been using earlier, turning it over in his hands with his back towards her. She felt as if a chasm separated them—an aching, yawning chasm that stood no chance of ever being bridged.

'It's a big step,' she said at last, her hands twisting in front of her in agitation. 'I…I'm not…not able to make it.'

His back remained turned towards her. She could see the outline of his muscles through his silk shirt, tense, as if poised in anger, and yet when he spoke his voice, surprisingly, held no trace of it.

'It's almost time for the party to begin.'

'Yes.'

Her teeth snagged her bottom lip as she waited for his next move. She wanted to explain, but couldn't think of the words to describe her innermost doubts and fears. There was so much he didn't know about her, and yet he knew her body so intimately, almost better than she knew it herself. But while her body responded to his so vulnerably her mind could not. She'd closed that part off to protect herself, and even though she wanted to free herself from the past it clung to her like an anklet of heavy steel. She just couldn't shake it off.

He put her hairbrush down and turned to face her. His expression gave nothing away; it was mask-like, shuttered. She wondered for a sickening moment if he'd tell her to get out of his life now that she'd reneged on the deal. She braced herself for the words, her back tight with tension, her legs unsteady, finding it impossible to hold his eyes with hers in case he saw the desperation reflected there.

'I'll see you downstairs,' he said, totally rocking her out of her silent reverie of panic. 'We'll talk about this later.'

She opened and closed her mouth, but he'd already left the room. She caught sight of her expression in the dressing table mirror and marvelled at how impassive she looked when inside she was crumbling. She picked up the tube of lipstick and reapplied it where her teeth had worried it off, the slight tremor of her hand as she did so the only outward clue to her disquietude.

CHAPTER NINE

CARA gave herself several minutes before she made the journey downstairs. The sound of clinking glasses and the happy chatter of the guests who'd already arrived came from the large formal lounge directly below. She slipped more or less unnoticed down the stairs, and was privately congratulating herself on avoiding a host of interested stares when she came face to face with Megan Fry.

'Hello, Cara.' Megan greeted her coolly, her eyes raking her from head to foot. 'I didn't think you were coming.'

'I changed my mind,' Cara said, making a move to pass.

One of Megan's cold hands touched her on the arm and Cara stopped, lifting one brow questioningly.

Megan's hand fell away, but her blue eyes remained icy and they met Cara's determinedly.

'I'm sure Byron would prefer it if we were friends,' she said. 'I am, after all, bringing your business back from the brink.'

Cara's scalp lifted at the cold, hard stare in Megan's washed-out blue eyes.

'I have enough friends.' She made to push past again and Megan stepped back. 'If you'll excuse me—'

'Cara?'

Byron's deep baritone stalled her. She looked up to see him standing with a glass of champagne in each hand, his eyes quickly assessing the situation.

'Yes?'

Her one word came out sharply and his eyebrow lifted.

'Please excuse me, Megan.' She addressed the other

woman in tones of forced politeness. 'I think I'm expected to mingle. Enjoy the party.'

Megan's smile didn't quite make the distance to her eyes. 'I will,' she answered, with a sultry glance towards Byron. 'Is that for me?' She scooped the glass of champagne out of his hand and with another suggestive wink swept past to join the other guests.

Byron waited until they were alone to ask, 'What was all that about?'

'What was all what about?'

He nodded in the direction Megan had gone. 'You don't like her, do you?'

'Am I supposed to like her?' she asked with a tight edge to her voice.

'It would makes things a whole lot easier if you did,' he answered.

'Well, I'm sorry to be so uncooperative, but if you don't mind I'd like to choose both my own friends and my business associates.'

'As far as I can see you don't have any particularly close friends and you don't appear to be all that choosy over your business associates either,' he observed dryly.

'You know nothing of my social life,' she shot back.

'What social life?'

She straightened her back in anger. 'I like my own company, there's nothing wrong with that.'

'You remind me of a nun,' he said, taking a sip of his drink. 'Cloistered away from possible temptation. Shut off from the real world in case you get hurt.'

Cara's jaw ached with the tension of keeping her temper under some sort of civil control. She was conscious of the background chatter of the party guests in the next room, and imagined it wouldn't go down terribly well if she were to let fly right here and now.

'What I don't understand is why you're taking the Pill?'

he added before she could speak. 'Why bother? Or did you just do it to get back at me?'

'I've been on the pill for years.' Her voice came out hard and flat. 'I have terrible periods. Don't you remember?'

His eyes softened.

'Yes, I do remember.'

Cara tore her eyes away from his with an effort. A vision of him tucking her into bed with a hot water bottle after their fourth date flitted into her mind. He'd been so gentle, so understanding. He'd waved away her embarrassment, reminding her he had both a sister and a mother, that he was no stranger to the intimate shifts of a woman's body.

'Your parents will wonder where I've got to…' she began uncertainly.

'Cara, I think we should—'

Just then the lounge door opened wide and Fliss poked her head out.

'Come on, you two,' she called. 'Dad's just about to start his welcoming speech.'

Cara found herself being swept into the proceedings as if she'd never been away. No one seemed to be in the least surprised to hear her introduced as Byron's partner for the evening, although she was conscious of the slight sneer lurking about Megan's mouth as Byron led her towards a great-aunt she'd not met before.

Great-Aunt Milly grasped Cara's hand in her paper-thin one and smiled broadly.

'I didn't get to meet you the first time around.' The soft wrinkles on her face met as she smiled. 'Better late than never, eh?'

'Yes.' Cara smiled hesitantly.

'Come and sit here beside me.' Great-Aunt Milly patted the seat next to her. 'Since I broke my hip I can't stand for too long. I've had three, you know.'

'Broken hips?' Cara stared at her in empathic alarm.

'Good God, no.' Aunt Milly chuckled. 'Husbands, my dear. I've had three.'

'Oh.' Cara glanced towards Byron for help, but he'd moved on to speak with another guest.

'They're all dead now.'

'I'm sorry…'

'Oh, don't be,' Aunt Milly said briskly. 'I'm not. Shouldn't have married any of 'em.'

'I…'

Aunt Milly gave her a mischievous wink as she leaned towards her, her almost black eyes sparkling.

'So you've finally come to your senses and gone back to Byron, have you?'

'I—'

'He's the pick of the litter, of course,' she continued, almost without a pause. 'Always said he was. Reminds me of a man I once loved.'

'One of your husbands?' Cara offered.

Great-Aunt Milly shook her head.

'Didn't love any of them. I married each of them for their money. No, the love of my life I stupidly let get away.'

Cara was intrigued. She found herself leaning closer to the old woman, her eyes wide with interest.

Great-Aunt Milly obviously loved playing to an audience. Her dark eyes twinkled at the expression on Cara's face.

'You're shocked by me, aren't you?'

'I—'

'Most people are,' she continued, as if she hadn't heard Cara's tiny squeak. 'But I kind of figure that if at eighty-nine I don't say what I mean to say, I mightn't get another chance. Every day is a bonus after seventy, or so they say. You want to make the most of your young life. All too soon you'll be looking in the mirror and wondering who that old crow is, only to find out it's actually you. I nearly had a heart attack on the spot after I got my cataracts done. Not only did I look like a dried-up prune, but the white dove I'd been feeding for months on my front lawn turned out to be a seagull! Think of it! Here I was, telling everyone God was giving me a sign and all the time it was a pesky scavenging seagull!'

Cara laughed out loud. The sound of her amused tinkling turned several heads, including her ex-husband's.

'Is he good in bed?' Great-Aunt Milly winked at her, noticing Byron's quick glance.

Cara's mouth fell open.

'No point continuing if he isn't,' the old lady rambled on. 'I know about these things. I'm what you'd call experienced. A woman will forgive a lot if her man is a tiger in bed.'

'I…I…'

'Hasn't he reacquainted you yet with his talent?' She poked a long gnarled finger at Cara's slim arm. 'He's not the man I thought he was if he hasn't. Mind you, that Fry girl is all over him like a bad case of psoriasis. Had that once. Worse thing that ever happened to me other than my three husbands. At least when my husbands died I had their money. After a bout of psoriasis all I was left with was scars. I scratched myself silly. No self-control; that's the problem.'

Cara giggled, her own self-control slipping.

'I've never met anyone like you before,' she confessed.

'What?' Great-Aunt Milly frowned at her playfully. 'No one as old, do you mean?'

Cara's smile transformed her face as she faced Byron's engaging relic of a relative.

'Someone so honest.'

'Oh.' Great-Aunt Milly shrugged off the compliment. 'As I said, honesty is the only thing you have left when you get to my age. All my friends have either died or succumbed to dementia. No point in pretending any more. I speak as I find and I don't give a damn. I did once, but not now.' She gave Cara an eagle-eyed look before adding, 'You still love him, don't you?'

Cara rolled her lips together, stalling for time.

'Oh.' Great-Aunt Milly waved a dismissive hand towards her. 'Go on, deny it. I know that's the fashionable thing to do. Young women don't like to make themselves vulnerable any more. I'm all for the Women's Movement, don't get me wrong, but somehow we women have shot ourselves in the foot. I know what I'm talking about, girl. I woke up on my fiftieth birthday and my biological clock chose exactly that moment to go off with a bang. Too late. Far too late. And there was nothing I could do about it.'

'I...'

'I would've loved a son like Byron,' Great-Aunt Milly continued dreamily. 'Someone strong and dependable. He visits me regularly, you know. None of the others do. Felicity did once, but only because she needed money. I sent her packing, of course. I might be old but I'm not a fool. She came to her senses and threw herself back into Jason's arms. He's a nice boy. A bit shy, but it's the quiet ones you have to watch. Felicity looks satisfied now, though. I like to think I brought that about.'

'I'm sure she's very happy...'

'So...' Great-Aunt Milly leaned even closer. 'Will you have his baby now?'

Cara reared back in shock.

'I...I'm not sure I—'

'Don't dilly-dally like I did. Get on with it. He'll make a good father, I'm sure of that.'

'I'm not sure I'd be a very good mother,' Cara said cautiously. 'I don't have what it takes.' Her heart squeezed painfully at the ironic truth of those words.

Great-Aunt Milly's eyes darted back to hers.

'Don't be ridiculous, girl,' she said. 'You've got so much

banked-up love in you any kid would be glad to have you as its parent. Didn't your mother tell you that?'

'My mother hated me,' Cara stated flatly. 'That's what she told me.'

Great-Aunt Milly frowned and her wrinkles intermingled again.

'I'm starting to see the fine print,' she said. 'Have you told Byron?'

Cara shrugged defeatedly.

'He wouldn't understand. He's got two parents who love him. I didn't even have one.'

'Your father absconded?'

'He died before I was born.'

'Well…' Great-Aunt Milly eyeballed her once again. 'What do you think he might've felt about you?'

'I don't know. My mother didn't tell me much. I think she blamed me for his death in some way. He was out drinking with friends. It was late at night and he didn't have a hope. No seatbelts, no second chances. My mother hinted once or twice that he'd been out celebrating the fact he'd just become a father, that if it hadn't been for me he'd still be alive.'

A small silence fell between them. Cara was conscious of the all-seeing dark, spirited gaze that so reminded her of Byron's.

'Have I shocked you?' Cara borrowed Great-Aunt Milly's earlier question.

The old lady shook her head.

'Not much shocks me these days,' she said. 'But you don't have to follow your mother's blueprint, you know. Lots of people turn out to be wonderful parents themselves, even though they've suffered dreadful abuse from their own.'

'I can't take the risk.' She didn't say why. No one but she knew why.

'Life is full of risks. You can go to the fair and only ride on the merry-go-round, and go round and round in circles, or you can get on the rollercoaster and feel the rush of the wind in your hair and the drop of your stomach on the way down. Both are fun, but I know which one I'd prefer.'

Cara smiled at the thought of Byron's elderly great-aunt screaming her head off on a rollercoaster. Great-Aunt Milly grinned back at her.

'Don't let life pass you by, my dear. If I were you I'd take Byron back on any terms, otherwise someone else will.' With that she gave a quick toss of her white-crowned head in Megan Fry's direction.

Cara turned her gaze to where Megan had draped herself along the back of the single chair Byron was sitting on as he talked to someone alongside.

Byron looked up, as if he'd sensed her eyes on him, and, excusing himself, rose out of the chair and came back to where she and Great-Aunt Milly were sitting.

'Another drink, Aunt Milly?' he asked, taking her empty glass.

'Yes, dear boy. A double brandy and dry.'

'What about you, Cara?' His eyes turned towards her, his mouth lifting slightly at one corner.

'No, I'm fine.'

He went to fetch his aunt's drink and Great-Aunt Milly leaned towards her once more with a conspiratorial whisper.

'Never could resist a tall man myself.' Her dark eyes twinkled at Cara. 'And they don't come much taller than that outside of an American basketball team, now, do they?'

Cara looked at the tall figure of her ex-husband as he organised the drinks and sighed.

'No,' she said softly. 'They don't.'

The evening continued noisily and more and more guests rolled up. Cara found herself being eyeballed by Leon and Olivia's three children as they stood some distance from her.

Ben, the eldest at seven, was periodically nudged by his five-year-old sister Bethany, who had obviously appointed him official spokesperson. Clare, at three, was sucking her thumb rather vigorously as she surveyed the party through eyes so like her uncle's Cara felt a sensation almost like pain in the region of her stomach.

She decided to put the poor boy out of his misery. She left her mineral water on the coffee table and approached the little group.

'Hi, I'm Cara. You must be Ben, Bethany and Clare.'

Three young faces smiled up at her.

'Are you still our aunty?' Bethany asked. 'Katie said you are.'

Cara couldn't help smiling at the forthright family likeness. It seemed that Great-Aunt Milly had a lot to answer for genetically.

'I think I might be,' she answered.

'That's good,' Ben said shyly.

Cara bent down to Clare's level. The chocolate-brown eyes blinked back at her, the thumb staying put in the tiny rosebud mouth.

'Hello, Clare.'

'Bwello,' the little tot answered around her thumb.

'She's not supposed to do that any more,' Bethany said with all the authority of an older sister *in loco parentis*. 'Mummy said.'

'Have you three had something to eat?' Cara asked as she took Clare's unoccupied chubby hand. 'I was just going to find a sausage roll or two. Want to help me hunt them down?'

Bethany took Cara's other hand and tugged.

'I know where they are!' she said excitedly. 'Granny gave me one before.'

It wasn't long before Cara was surrounded by both children and crumbs. Katie and Kirstie had joined them, and were now sitting on the floor in front of Cara with Bethany. Clare was on her knee and Ben was leaning against the arm of Cara's chair, his grey-blue eyes lighting up when his mother approached.

'I hope everyone is behaving themself over here,' Olivia said, and, lifting her gaze to Cara, added, 'You're a kid magnet, Cara, but you don't have to be on crowd control all evening. Go and find Byron and have some fun.'

'I am having fun.'

Olivia gave her a warm, friendly smile.

'Byron's right,' she said. 'You'll make a great mother.'

Before Cara could think of a reply Olivia had already disappeared back into the crowd of guests.

'Are you going to have a baby?' Katie asked.

'I...'

'She can't,' Kirstie said. 'She's not married to Uncle Byron any more.'

'Yes, she can,' Bethany piped up. 'My friend Jenny's mum isn't married to her boyfriend, and they're having a baby at Christmas.'

'Why don't you get married again?' Katie asked Cara. 'To Uncle Byron?'

'Katie, it's none of your business,' Ben said quietly.

'What would you know?' Katie's tone was scathing. 'You're just a boy.'

'Uncle Byron doesn't want to get married again,' he said with solemn authority. 'I heard him tell Daddy.'

Cara felt sick. She knew she should lure the children towards another topic, but couldn't organise her brain enough to summon up the words to do so.

A shadow fell across her face and she looked up to see Megan Fry, drink in hand, one hip tilted arrogantly, her expression derisory.

'Quite the little domestic, aren't you?' she said, with a

sugar-sweet smile that Cara was sure was solely for the children's benefit.

'Enjoying the party?' Cara offered politely.

Megan's eyes swept over the children's faces cursorily. She bent down, patted the twins on the head and, straightening once more, gave Cara a cold stare.

'It won't work, you know.'

'Excuse me?' Cara lifted one brow in query.

Megan's mouth tightened and, giving the children another sweeping glance, leaned towards her to whisper, 'Your little ploy to win him back. It's not going to work.'

'I have no idea what you're talking about,' Cara said, holding Clare protectively against her chest. The little tot had fallen asleep, thumb still in residence. The other children by this time had wandered off in search of drinks, much to Cara's relief; somehow she didn't think what Megan had to say was for tender ears.

'You can't give him what he wants,' Megan said. 'But I can and I will.'

'I won't stand in your way,' Cara answered with a quiet calm she was secretly proud of. Inside she was crumbling at the threat behind the other woman's words. Surely she didn't know the real reason Cara couldn't fulfil Byron's terms? But then Megan had a stealthy determination about her that Cara hadn't recognised before. It occurred to her that perhaps Megan was prepared to go to incredible lengths to achieve her aims—further than a more morally engaged person would go.

'Sensible of you,' Megan answered. 'But I'll feel happier when you're out of his house.'

'What about his bed?' Cara's eyes sparked with a challenge of her own. 'Is that off limits too?'

Megan's face was almost puce with anger. She opened her mouth to say something, but just then Fliss waddled over, interrupting the tense little tableau.

'You've just got to have some of these,' she said, waving a plate of elegantly assembled sushi towards Cara.

'Mmm,' Cara took one and popped it in her mouth.

'What about you, Megan?' Fliss brandished the plate under Megan's nose. 'Fancy some raw fish?'

Megan looked as if she was going to be sick.

'No,' she said on a choked gasp. 'Excuse me...'

Once she'd gone Fliss licked her fingers and put the plate on one of the side tables before taking the chair beside Cara. Cara watched as she wriggled into a comfortable position, her hands coming to rest on the taut mound of her belly.

'What did Megan want?' Fliss asked.

Cara hesitated. She didn't want to be the one to burst the Rockcliffe bubble where Megan was concerned.

'Nothing much.'

Fliss gave her a wry look.

'You can tell me. I know what she's up to.'

Cara gave her a startled glance.

'You do?'

Fliss nodded and stroked her belly once more. Cara watched in fascination as a tiny foot-shaped lump appeared under the tight drum of Fliss's clothing.

'Want a feel?'

She took Cara's free hand and placed it on the wriggling foot.

'Wow!' Her eyes were wide as she met Fliss's amused gaze. 'Doesn't that hurt?'

Fliss smiled.

'Not half as much as it's going to in a few short weeks.'

Cara returned her hand to stroke Clare's back, where she still lay snuggled against her.

'Are...are you nervous?'

Fliss shook her head.

'Not really. I believe in using drugs—lots of them. I was so out of it when Thomas was born—high as a kite, in fact.

No sense in suffering unnecessarily. I felt three contractions and immediately called for help.'

Cara couldn't help smiling at Fliss's matter-of-factness. Great-Aunt Milly's blood had certainly got around!

Fliss swivelled in her seat, her eyes holding Cara's.

'Don't let Megan win this.'

Cara swallowed.

'Win what?'

Fliss gave her a long, assessing look before speaking.

'Megan is desperate to tie Byron to her. She'll do anything to bring it about.'

'Anything?'

Fliss gave her another long look.

'Some people go to the most extraordinary lengths to achieve their goals. Don't forget I've studied just about every personality type on earth. Megan will stop at nothing to get what she wants.'

Cara forced her features into impassivity as she returned Fliss's direct gaze.

'Then it's very fortunate that Megan and I don't want the same thing, isn't it?'

'Are you sure about that, Cara?' Fliss asked. 'Really sure?'

Cara's eyes shifted to the sleeping child in her lap.

'I've never been more certain of anything in my life.'

There was an awkward little silence.

'He doesn't love her, you know,' Fliss stated baldly.

'He must feel something for her,' Cara managed to say, with an outward calm she was privately proud of. 'She's been a part of his life ever since they shared a bath. Now she's working for him as well. It would certainly be a convenient move on both their parts to formalise their relationship.'

Fliss rolled her lips together thoughtfully.

'Look, I realise you're an only child, and the intimacy of

family life is something outside of your experience, but even Leon and Patrick have shared a bath with her. She was here all the time while we were growing up. My mother and hers went to school together. Since Stella died Mum has more or less adopted Megan.'

'Even more reason for me to get out of the picture.'

'No,' Fliss insisted. 'Everyone is so over the "Megan must marry Byron" phase.'

'Everyone, that is, except Megan,' Cara pointed out dryly.

Fliss's smooth brow furrowed.

'Don't you care about him any more?' she asked.

Cara lowered her gaze, concentrating on the silken head still resting against her breast.

'What I feel or don't feel is irrelevant to this conversation,' she said.

Fliss threw her a disdainful look and struggled to her feet.

'I used to so admire you, Cara,' she said. 'I thought you were courageous and strong, but you're not. You'd rather throw away your own happiness than face a confrontation. What the hell happened to you?'

Cara fought against the sting of tears at the back of her eyes. Her voice, however, was devoid of emotion as she looked at Byron's sister across the top of the sleeping child's head.

'Life happened.'

The tense moment was interrupted by the approach of Jason. He slipped an arm around his wife's middle and greeted Cara warmly. Cara was so grateful for the reprieve that her own greeting bordered on the effusive. With a hard little look Cara's way, Fliss excused herself with needing the bathroom.

'Where's your little boy?' Cara broke the small silence that had fallen between them on Fliss's exit.

'He's asleep,' Jason informed her. 'Like all good children should be.' He indicated the sleeping bundle in her arms.

Cara smiled and stroked the little girl's back.

'I knew my boring old personality would come to some use some time,' she quipped.

Another silence fell. Cara was almost certain Jason was going to ask her what her little tiff with Fliss had been about. She was busily rehearsing a parcel of lies when he asked instead, 'Can I get you a drink or something?'

She opened her mouth to reply just as Olivia joined them.

'Here.' Olivia reached down for her daughter. 'I'll pop her into bed so you can circulate a bit. Thanks so much for looking after her. Ben and Bethany think you're a genius because Clare usually cries for half an hour before going to sleep.'

Cara gave Jason an I-told-you-I-was-boring glance as she handed Clare over.

'Thomas down?' Olivia asked her brother-in-law.

'Out for the count.'

'Two down and four to go,' Olivia said with a grin.

'I promised to finish a story for Katie and Kirstie,' Cara said, getting to her feet.

'They're still partying,' Olivia said. 'Jase, get Cara a drink and make her relax. I don't know where Byron's got to. Have you seen him?'

'I think he's taking Megan back to her hotel. She wasn't feeling very well,' Jason answered.

'Oh?' Olivia's expression was speculative. 'I wonder what brought that on.'

Cara felt in no mood to contribute to the discussion, so, excusing herself, made her way towards the kitchen in search of a glass of water. She was just passing the small breakfast room off the kitchen when she heard her name spoken. Despising herself for listening, and yet unable to stop herself, she stood just outside the door, pretending to be interested in the family portrait in front of her in the hall.

'...terrible when you think of it,' an older female voice

was saying. 'She left him after only four months of marriage. One of Byron's friends saw her a couple of months later, looking suspiciously pregnant, but when he caught sight of her two weeks later she was flat as a pancake.'

'Oh?' The other voice lifted with increasing intrigue. 'Don't tell me she had an...'

A word Cara couldn't quite catch passed between them, but she knew without hearing exactly what it was.

CHAPTER TEN

THE picture in front of her blurred and her fingertips started to tingle as if she was going to pass out.

'How dreadful!' another voice chimed in, obviously relishing the juicy gossip. 'What a shameless hussy, to come back in the family fold as if butter wouldn't melt in her mouth. She must be after his money. He's loaded, you know. His property developing business has really taken off in the last few years.'

'Oh, I'm sure it's all about money,' the original speaker said with hardened cynicism. 'Isn't it always?'

'Well, she won't be around the family for too long once she hears Megan Fry's news.'

'What news is that?'

Cara felt as if her ears were stretching in their effort to hear every torturous word, but nothing could have prepared her for the shock of what was coming next.

'She's having a baby—*his* baby.'

'Byron's?' The older of the two voices sounded surprised. 'Are you sure?'

'Who else's could it be?' the other one answered confidently.

Cara didn't stay to hear any more. She spun on her heel and cannoned straight into the rock-hard wall of a very male chest.

'Interesting relatives, aren't they?' Byron said, steadying her with strong hands.

Cara opened and closed her mouth and wondered how long he'd been standing there. Had he heard?

'Y...yes.' She flicked a glance towards the portrait she'd

128

been looking at sightlessly. 'Who's the artist? Anyone famous?' she rambled as she peered at the signature, but her eyes were stubbornly uncooperative.

'My great-grandfather painted it,' Byron said from behind her left shoulder. 'Great-Aunt Milly found it in her attic and kindly passed it on.'

'It's very…' She hunted for a suitable adjective but all she could come up with was, 'Er…nice.'

'Have you eaten?' he asked.

She could feel his body warmth as he stood in front of her. It made her feel breathless and disorientated.

'No, I—'

'Come on, then.' He took her arm. 'I just got a glimpse of the dessert table. Let's go and help ourselves before it's all gone.'

'I'm not all that hungry…'

'You're not sick, are you?' He looked at her closely. 'Megan's come down with a bug. I just took her back to her hotel. Perhaps it's the same thing.'

'I can assure you it's not.' She couldn't quite conceal the bitterness in her tone.

He gave her another assessing look.

'Is everything all right?'

Cara lifted her chin.

'What could possibly be wrong?'

'I don't know.' His hold on her arm relaxed into a gentle caress. 'You seem a little on edge.'

Cara couldn't believe her ears.

'And why would that be?'

'I don't know,' he said again. 'You tell me. Did Great-Aunt Milly upset you?'

'No, of course not. I like her. She's the most honest Rockcliffe I've met so far.'

'What's that supposed to mean?'

'Go figure.'

He sighed in exasperation.

'Look, if you're upset about me taking Megan home, don't be.'

'That's very reassuring,' she bit out caustically. 'It's not unlike the stable hand locking the door once the horses have bolted.'

'What?' He frowned at her in puzzlement.

'You heard.'

'You're jealous,' he said. 'Look, she did kiss me once, but that was all; unfortunately my nieces witnessed it. Megan is a family friend. We—'

'More family than friend, I'd say,' she interjected.

'What's all this about?' he asked. 'Is all this because I employed her to fix your business? Is that what this is?'

Cara gave him a frosty glance.

'Employ who you like. It makes no difference to me. I'm looking for another job once I get back to Sydney anyhow.' She swung out of his hold and with quickened steps made her way back to the crush of guests in the formal lounge.

It was soon time for the cake and speeches. Cara stood to one side and wondered how she'd ended up in such a farcical situation. Her ex-husband was going to be a father to a child by his childhood sweetheart and there was nothing she could do about it. Pain wrenched at her insides like knives in tender flesh. How could she bear it?

'...and I'd like to thank my adorable wife, Jan, who's done a marvellous job of bringing up our four children. And I'd like to thank our four children. Byron, Patrick, Leon and Felicity...'

Cara could stand no more. She slipped away during the riotous applause over one of Rob's jokes and made her way outside into the garden.

The moon was a suspended sickle in the inky sky, a sprinkling of stars adorning its surrounds. The night breeze held a hint of jasmine and orange blossom and she breathed deeply, looking for solace.

'I thought I'd find you out here.' Byron spoke from behind her.

She didn't turn to face him, instead kept looking up at the night sky.

He came to stand alongside her. She felt the brush of his shoulder against her and caught a faint whiff of his after-shave when a tiny breeze brushed past her face, carrying his scent to her.

'You don't like crowds, do you?' he asked after a long silence.

Cara shifted so his face came into view. The lights from the terrace cast his features in shadow, but she could still make out his wry half-smile.

'I'm sure no one will miss me.'

'On the contrary.' His smile tilted a little more. 'I missed you.'

She didn't know what to make of his simple comment. A vision of Megan flitted into her mind, her belly ripe with the child he craved.

She lifted her chin determinedly and faced him full on.

'Byron, this arrangement we have has to stop. Immediately.'

His brow creased, his eyes darkly hooded.

'Why? Because of Megan?'

She gave an exasperated sound in the back of her throat.

'Of course because of Megan.'

He disturbed his hair with his hand. Even in shadow she could see his expression was troubled. Serve him right, she thought to herself. Let him sweat out this dilemma of his own making.

'I know I should have told you I was employing her as business manager, but I didn't want to put you off. I thought once you got to know her properly you'd see how talented she really is—'

'Oh, she's very talented,' Cara shot back before he could finish. 'There's no question about that.'

'So what's the problem?'

'The problem is I don't play second fiddle to anyone.'

'I'm not asking you to play second fiddle. I'm asking you—no, I'm telling you that Megan is your best chance at getting your business back on its feet once more. She's highly qualified in business management. I've seen her work and it's highly commendable.'

'I want out,' she said. 'I no longer have any interest in the business.'

'Now you're being ridiculous.'

'Am I?' She gave him a hard look, her eyes flashing defiantly. 'I'm not some piece on a chessboard you can shift around at will. I don't play those games any more. Buy me out. Perhaps Megan would like to purchase my share of the business. It might come in handy some time in the future, when she wants to take maternity leave.'

'You really hate her, don't you?'

Cara gave him a disbelieving look. What did he expect her to feel?

'Look,' she said tightly, 'I don't care quite how you go about setting up your stud of Rockcliffes, but count me out. This brood mare is out for a spell.'

She spun on her high heels and headed back towards the brightly lit house.

'Cara!'

His voice rang out insistently behind her, but she kept going regardless, immensely relieved when Jan appeared on the terrace and greeted her warmly.

'Cara, the twins are insisting on you tucking them into bed. Be an angel?'

'Of course.'

It was a welcome reprieve, even if she had to think on her feet for a story suitably entertaining for young ears. She didn't think Katie and Kirstie's parents would thank her for disillusioning their daughters with the perfidy of men—in particular that of their very own uncle.

'...and the only thing she could think of was to imagine herself far away. She could see herself riding high upon the fluffily white clouds. And when the sun went down the stars would light her way. They were like millions of tiny diamonds, shining down for her to find her way through to the land of her dreams.'

Cara looked down at the rapt little faces around her.

'And?' Katie prodded.

Care smiled and continued, 'The land of the little girl's dreams was far, far away. She needed much more than stars to help her to find it. She needed magic.'

'What sort of magic?' Kirstie asked.

'The sort of magic you have to go looking for,' Cara said. 'It's mostly hidden. That's because there's only a certain amount to go around all the people in the world. You have to know where to look.'

'Where do you have to look?' Katie asked, her eyes wide with interest.

'Inside yourself,' Cara answered. 'The magic is within you. All the magic you ever need is right inside you. You just have to believe in yourself to get to it.'

'Did the unhappy little girl find it?' Kirstie asked.

'Eventually,' Cara lied. 'But it took a long time and a lot of soul-searching before she finally let go of the past and embraced the future.' She patted the bed beside them. 'Come on, you two. Time for bed. It's after eleven p.m. I can't have you turning into pumpkins, now, can I?'

'I love the story of Cinderella!' Kirstie piped up. 'Can you tell us that?'

Cara shook her head.

'If you don't go to sleep within the next few minutes I'll be the one who turns into a pumpkin—or, worse still, the wicked stepmother!'

The twins giggled as they settled underneath the covers.

'I like your stories,' Katie said, throwing her chubby arms around Cara's neck affectionately.

'I love that you're our aunty again,' Kirstie said, doing the same.

Cara swallowed the lump in her throat and tucked them both in.

'I love being your aunty,' she said with a husky catch in her voice. 'Goodnight.'

The party was still in full swing downstairs. Cara slipped in to the lounge room, where coffee and liqueurs were being served. She refused offers from both Patrick and Leon and instead found a vacant seat next to Great-Aunt Milly.

'I'm drunk,' Great-Aunt Milly said baldly. 'I've had far too much brandy, and after the champagne with the speeches I'm well and truly pickled.'

Cara just smiled. The sharp bird-like gaze before her gave absolutely no indication whatsoever of inebriation.

'I never could hold my liquor,' Great-Aunt Milly continued as Cara settled herself in the chair beside her. 'I'm sure it was invented by men as a means to get women to do what they want.'

'You're probably right,' Cara conceded.

Great-Aunt Milly looked over her with an eagle eye.

'I saw you with the children,' she said. 'You're a natural.'

Cara gave a tentative smile.

'They're nice kids.'

'They're brats,' Great-Aunt Milly stated emphatically. 'Especially that little madam Katie. You did well to get them under some sort of control. God knows, Patrick and Sally haven't managed to do it so far.'

'She's definitely outspoken.' Cara gave her a teasing glance. 'But isn't that a Rockcliffe trait?'

Great-Aunt Milly gave her a hooded look from underneath eyebrows that hadn't seen a pair of tweezers for decades.

'Perhaps you're right.' The dark eyes twinkled with amusement. 'I've always thought a bit of spunk was a good thing.'

'It will certainly help her in the long run,' Cara said, looking down at her hands.

'Yes,' Great-Aunt Milly replied, her look long and encompassing. 'It will.'

Finally the grand old house began to empty of its guests, leaving only the family members who were staying the night to do a general tidy-up before collapsing into bed.

'I'm bushed,' Jan Rockcliffe said, flopping into a vacant chair. 'I don't remember our wedding day being as exhausting as this!'

'Our wedding day was forty years ago,' Byron's father pointed out. 'We were a whole lot younger and energetic back then.'

'You two go to bed,' Byron said, giving his mother a hand out of the chair. 'We'll do a quick tidy and the rest we'll leave for Mrs Timsby in the morning.'

His parents didn't refuse.

Patrick and Sally soon followed, and Leon and Olivia made a token effort to collect a few glasses before disappearing as well. Jason had already tucked Fliss into bed, and after helping to wash a few things he too made his departure.

Cara wondered if everyone's exit was for her benefit. Perhaps Byron's family thought she needed some time alone with him? But the very last thing she wanted was to be left in his company, unprotected from the temptation of his arms. Even knowing what she now knew about his relationship with Megan didn't stop her traitorous body from responding to the proximity of his. She'd been fighting it all evening.

The brush of his arm against hers now, as they each reached for a stray glass or plate, the clash of their gazes across the room, brief but telling, the fragrance of his aftershave as he moved past her...

'That's enough,' he said, breaking into her thoughts. 'We'll leave the rest till morning. It's nearly two a.m.'

Cara shut the dishwasher and dried her hands on a teatowel before she faced him.

'I'll go to bed, then,' she said. 'Goodnight.'

'Cara?'

Her hands momentarily stilled on the teatowel she was hanging against the cooker.

'Yes?'

'I'll be with you in a minute.'

She gave him a speaking glance.

'You have your own bed,' she said, injecting sarcasm into her tone. 'Surely you don't require mine as well?'

His look was steady, but she could see latent anger lurking in the depths of his dark eyes.

'I made a promise to you earlier,' he said. 'We have some unfinished business, if you remember.'

'I haven't forgotten, but I have changed my mind. Have you forgotten? This arrangement is off. *Finito*. The baby-making enterprise has been grounded.'

His eyes followed the agitated movement of her hands as she spoke. Cara thrust them by her sides and glared back at him defiantly.

'Why must you constantly throw obstacles across the pathway of what we both want?' he asked with bitterness. 'You wanted me this morning. It would take me less than five minutes to make you want me again.'

Cara lifted her chin a fraction.

'How long does it take with Megan?'

Byron's mouth tightened.

'So we're back to that, are we?'

'It's proving to be rather a stumbling block, yes,' she said with heavy irony.

He gave an exasperated sound at the back of his throat.

'Nothing I say will change what you think, will it?'

She shrugged.

'I've heard it virtually from the horse's mouth.'

'Megan?' he frowned.

'Let's say she's been marking her territory rather convincingly.'

'That's just Megan,' he said. 'She's very protective of my family.'

'And you in particular.'

He didn't deny it.

'Megan was there for me when you left,' he said after a slight pause. 'She listened while I raved and she soothed while I raged. I've done the same for her. She hasn't had much luck with relationships either.'

Cara hated hearing how Megan had inveigled her way into his life. She couldn't help thinking it had been deliberate, a specific plan to make him forget about her altogether.

'What a pity you didn't hook up with her in the first place,' she said. 'You could've saved yourself both money and grief, and pleased your whole family in the process.'

'My family have done all they can to welcome you, both in the past and now, and yet you persist in imagining they're against you.'

'Aren't they?'

'Of course not. It's not easy for them, I admit. When a couple goes through a divorce it's like dropping a stone in a pond. The ripples are far reaching. If they're a little guarded, particularly my mother, it's only because they don't want to see me hurt.'

'I'm sure Megan will help to salve any subsequent hurt you might feel once I get out of your life.'

'You are not going out of my life.' His tone was adamant.

'You might like to run that alongside Megan before you make it common knowledge,' Cara said. 'She has what is commonly referred to as a prior claim.'

He gave another frustrated sigh.

'Go to bed, Cara. You're acting like one of my nieces when they're overtired. You're not making any sense and it's pointless arguing with you.' With that he turned and left the room, leaving her to contemplate the empty room alone.

CHAPTER ELEVEN

CARA spent the rest of the night fighting with the bed-clothes. It was impossible to sleep when her mind was crawling with images of Megan and Byron's expected child. She tossed the pillow aside and turned to stare at the wooden panels of the closed door, her eyes smarting with tears she refused to allow to fall. She knew if she gave in to what she was feeling inside there would be no turning back. It had taken her this long to pull herself out of the abyss of despair that had accompanied her ever since she'd left Byron.

In keeping with her dour mood, the sun rose weakly in the east, shrouded by thick, turbulent clouds that carried a threat of thunder. Cara listened as the house gradually came to life, the children's voices carrying in the long halls.

She took her time showering, before making her way downstairs to where most of the family were gathered for breakfast.

'You look positively hungover,' Sally was saying to Byron as she poured coffee into his mug.

Byron gave a grunt that could have been either denial or agreement. Cara was conscious of several Rockcliffe glances pointed her way as she took the only vacant chair—next to Byron. His eyes flicked over her before returning to the dry toast in front of him.

'Coffee, Cara?' Sally hovered with the percolator.

Cara nodded and wished everyone would stop staring at her. She could feel a tide of colour steal into her cheeks as she caught the tail-end of Patrick's studied gaze resting on her.

'It was a great party,' Olivia said, breaking the tense silence. 'Great-Aunt Milly certainly enjoyed herself.'

'Excuse me.' Byron's chair scraped backwards, and, tossing his unused napkin aside, he left the room.

Cara could feel every pair of eyes on her.

'Toast, Cara?' Jan made a valiant effort to ease the tension in the room.

'No, thank you,' she said getting to her feet. 'If you'll excuse me…?'

'Are Uncle Byron and Auntie Cara having a fight?' Katie asked in a stage whisper to her mother.

Cara didn't stay to hear the reply. She went back to her room and methodically packed her things, lingering over the task to fill in time.

There was a gentle tap at the door and Cara opened it to find Fliss standing outside, her expression remorseful.

'I've come to apologise for last night,' she said, stepping into the room.

'There's no need…' Cara began.

'No, I was out of line.' Fliss sat on the bed with a sigh. 'It's this pregnancy—it's wreaking havoc on my emotions.'

'It's all right.'

'Don't be so gracious,' she said. 'I've spent most of the morning rehearsing this, so don't let it go to waste.'

Cara couldn't help a small smile. Fliss had always been a perfectionist, and she could easily imagine her spending hours working and reworking her speech.

'OK, then,' Cara said. 'Fire away.'

Fliss inspected her hands before lifting her gaze to Cara's.

'You might not believe this, but I was truly devastated when you left Byron. I missed you, and blamed myself that somehow I'd caused trouble.'

'No—'

'I was young and used to being the centre of attention with three big brothers. I wasn't used to sharing any of them, especially Byron. I took up so much of your time in those early days of your marriage. We all did. It's a Rockcliffe thing, I guess. Jason's always telling me how suffocating it can be.'

'I don't think—'

'It *is* suffocating,' Fliss said. 'Everyone knows everyone's business and there's no privacy. I'm so used to it I can barely see it happening, but I've been thinking about it a lot lately. You didn't stand a chance. We took over your life, trying too hard to make you feel part of the family when what you really needed was time alone with Byron.'

'Fliss, this is—'

'No, let me finish. Byron is so unhappy, and so are you.'

'He has Megan now.'

'She's not right for him.'

'Surely that's up to them to decide?' Cara said.

'No, it's up to you.'

'It has nothing whatsoever to do with me.'

'It has everything to do with you,' Fliss insisted. 'Byron needs to sort out the past before he can move on to the future. So do you.'

'Is this what you learnt in your degree?' Cara asked tightly. 'To speculate on people's private lives and neatly sort out all their hang-ups?'

'Cara, I've spent enough time around broken people to recognise your unhappiness. You're stuck in a deep groove of pain. It's as if you think you deserve to suffer, punishing yourself because of past mistakes or because of what your mother did to you.'

'I don't wish to speak of my mother. Now, if you'll excuse me, I want to finish packing.'

'Cara, you can't hide your head in the sand for ever. Byron told me—'

'He had no right!' Cara swung around angrily to glare at

Fliss. 'He knows nothing of what it was like. Nothing. And I don't want to ever discuss this again. Please leave.'

'Cara, please.' Fliss's eyes shone with tears. 'Don't throw away what could be your last chance at happiness, what could be Byron's last chance.'

Cara's mouth tightened. Her hands were balled fists by her sides and her hazel eyes glittered with anger.

'Go back to your perfect life, Felicity, and leave me alone. You're so like Byron it's unbelievable. You think you can wave a magic wand and start again, but life isn't like that. I've suffered. I've really suffered. And the only way I can survive is to lock it away where no one can see it. You have no right to meddle in my life. No right at all.'

'I have every right,' Fliss said in a placating tone. 'I care about you.'

'Do you?' Cara asked bitterly. 'Do you really? Or is this just about playing happy families the Rockcliffe way?'

'Cara, please—'

'I don't wish to continue this discussion.'

'You still love him, don't you?'

'Get out!' Cara gritted her teeth.

'You love him, but you won't allow yourself to have him because you're so intent on punishing yourself. What did you do, Cara? Why do you hate yourself so much?'

Cara's face was white with pain. She clenched and un-clenched her fists and fought against the wave of nausea that threatened to consume her.

'Tell me, Cara.' Fliss's tone was gentle but determined. 'Tell me.'

Cara turned away, her slim back a rigid wall against the probe of Fliss's words.

'Tell me, Cara.'

'I can't.'

'You remind me of a princess locked up in a tower,' Fliss said. 'But the irony is the key is on the inside, with you.

Only you can unlock that door and taste freedom. No one else can do it for you.'

'I can never be free.'

'Only because you don't want to be. People live through the most appalling things and survive. Don't bury yourself alive in the rubble of your mother's dysfunctional behaviour. You're cheating yourself out of your biggest victory—rewriting the past and not allowing the pattern to continue.'

Cara thought about Fliss's words. How she so wanted to rewrite the past. But it was too late. Byron had already achieved his goal of a child and had no further need of her. His dark mood earlier seemed to suggest he was already cutting her out of his life.

'I appreciate your concern,' she said hollowly. 'I really do. But this isn't a fairy story. It's real life. I have to live with the consequences of my own and other people's behaviour, as we all do. I have to do it my way.'

'Even if it ruins your life in the process?' Fliss asked.

'That's no one's business but my own.'

Fliss got up off the bed with a sigh.

'I'd better go. Jason will be wondering what's happened to me.' She turned at the door, her hand hesitating on the knob. 'Promise me you'll think about what I said? About the key being on your side?'

Cara gave her a sad half-smile.

'The key was thrown away a long time ago,' she said.

The barbecue planned for lunch had to be abandoned when storm clouds exploded over the garden in flashes of lightning and deafening thunder. Mrs Timsby bustled about, cooking meat under the large kitchen grill and deftly tossing salads, while the family gathered for drinks in the library.

Cara sat to one side, trying not to look at Byron. He seemed to be avoiding her, taking a seat on the other side of the room rather than the one next to hers. She pretended she hadn't noticed but inside she felt raw. She knew she should never have come with him to Melbourne. Too many wounds had been reopened.

'What time is your flight?' Sally asked as she perched on the arm of Cara's chair.

'Five,' Cara answered.

'Tell me about the house. Byron said you're decorating it for him.'

'It's a very grand house,' Cara said. 'Nice harbour views. You know Byron—nothing but the best.'

Sally smiled.

'It's great that you're doing it for him. Quite frankly, I didn't think you would under the circumstances.'

'Byron can be very persuasive at times,' Cara commented wryly.

'Yes, like the rest of the Rockcliffe males.' Sally laughed. 'Mind you, I'm not complaining. Patrick's the best thing that ever happened to me.'

She took one of the nibbles off the coffee table and turned back to Cara.

'So, are you going to patch things up with him?'

'Excuse me?'

'Byron and you.' Sally took an audible bite of her cracker.

'I'm afraid there's someone else,' Cara said carefully.

Sally's eyes widened.

'There is?'

Cara nodded.

'Does Byron know?'

'Of course he knows,' Cara said. 'How could he not know?'

Sally shrugged.

'Men can be a bit thick sometimes,' she said. 'They usually only see what they want to see.' She reached for another cracker and chewed it thoughtfully. 'This weekend must have been very difficult for you.'

'It's had its moments.'

'I'm sorry about Katie's outspokenness. She doesn't think before she speaks.'

'She's only five,' Cara pointed out. 'Plenty of time to learn.'

'You're extremely gracious.'

'I was five once.'

'Yes, of course.'

Just then Jan announced that lunch was ready and the conversation came to a welcome end. Cara could barely hide her relief. As much as she liked Sally, she didn't want to encourage any confidences when she would so soon be out of Byron's life. There didn't seem to be any point.

Cara took the seat next to Byron, at Jan's insistence, and then wished she hadn't. Byron pointedly ignored her the whole time, making her feel increasingly uncomfortable. Never had she wished for a meal to be over so quickly.

When Katie spilt her pink lemonade across the table and into Cara's lap she felt like kissing her in gratefulness. It gave her a valid excuse to leave the table, which she did, with assurances that her skirt was fine and she'd be back as soon as she'd rinsed it.

Finally the afternoon was over. Patrick was driving them to the airport, picking up Megan on the way. Cara said her goodbyes and sat in the back of the car, wishing herself a million miles away.

Megan had lost her pale wan look and was positively glowing as she came out of her hotel on Byron's arm, smiling up at him girlishly. Cara tore her eyes away and examined the electronic window mechanism with fierce intent.

'Hello, Cara,' Megan said as she slid into the seat beside her. 'I hope you don't mind me bumping forward on to your flight. I was going on a later one, but I hate travelling alone. Much more fun to go together.'

'I don't mind at all,' Cara lied.

Megan monopolised the conversation all the way to the airport and then in the members' lounge. If Byron was annoyed by it he didn't show it. He smiled at her amusing anecdotes and addressed one or two comments her way. Cara sat and silently fumed.

The flight was delayed for forty minutes after boarding. Cara thought she would scream with the frustration of having Megan wedged between them, cooing up at Byron like a devoted puppy. To hide her annoyance she buried her head in a magazine and ground her teeth in silent fury.

Soon after arriving in Sydney Megan bade them farewell as she was going out with friends for a late supper. In a stoical silence Cara followed Byron to where he'd parked the car on Friday evening.

'I'll take that,' he said, reaching for her hand luggage.

Cara felt the warm brush of his fingers against hers and almost dropped the bag in her haste to remove her hand. His eyes hardened as they flicked to hers.

'You used not to find my touch so abhorrent.'

'You used not to freeze me out with stony silences,' she shot back irritably.

'I have nothing I wish to say to you.'

'Good. Fine by me.'

'Although I can think of one or two things I should have said a long time ago.'

'Go right ahead. I'm sure I can cope with it.'

'I'm not so sure about that. You're not such a great fan of the truth.'

'Try me. I suppose you're going to harp on about me not letting go of the past, like your sister did in her little psychoanalysis session this morning? Say what you like. See if I care.'

He shut the boot and strode to the driver's door. He started the car and backed out without a word. He waited until he'd paid the parking attendant before speaking again.

'I didn't ask Fliss to grill you, if that's what you're implying.'

'I'm not implying anything. I just want this weekend to be over.'

'I realise it was difficult for you,' he said a few moments later. 'But my parents really enjoyed having you there.'

'Yes, I was the light entertainment for all and sundry. The object of gossip and innuendo. The target of ill-timed confessions of what the children saw. Glad to be of service.'

'You're far too attached to the victim role.'

'And you're far too attached to the overbearing ex-husband role.'

'I wouldn't be your ex-husband if you'd faced this seven years ago,' he pointed out bitterly.

'No, of course you wouldn't. You'd be happily married to the ecstatic Megan, with a brood of Rockcliffe lookalikes about your ankles.'

'Let's keep Megan out of this conversation.'

'Why?'

'Because she's not relevant to it. This is about us.'

'Us?' She swivelled in her seat to stare at him. 'There is no "us". There's no point flogging a dead horse, and as dead horses go this one is really starting to stink.'

He thrust the car into gear savagely and roared into the next lane on the Harbour Bridge.

'You really know how to aim your kicks,' he said.

'I had a good teacher.'

'So it seems.'

Cara tightened her arms across her chest and stared out of the window.

'Are you serious about leaving the business?' he asked as he pulled into his driveway some time later.

'Deadly serious.'

'But why? You've put so much into it. Why throw it all away now?'

'I no longer feel committed, I want a change.'

'It's because of Megan, isn't it?'

She shrugged coolly.

'Do you want me to dismiss her?' he asked.

'Would you do that?' She turned to look at him.

'It would be difficult,' he said, drumming his fingers on the steering wheel. 'But if that's what you want, then—'

'No.'

'No?' His eyes meshed with hers.

'No. I want to have a change. My heart's not been in the business since…for quite some time.'

'What will you do?'

'I don't know,' she said, unclipping her seatbelt. 'I could go back to university, take up some sort of study. Psychology, perhaps.'

'One psychologist in the family is surely quite enough.'

'But I'm not in the family,' she said. 'Any more.'

He didn't answer. She followed him into the house and wondered if she'd annoyed him again. His mouth had tightened and his shoulders had hunched as if in tension. She couldn't work him out. Surely he should be relieved that she was leaving without a fuss. It would make his future life with Megan so much easier without her trailing after him in lovelorn despondency.

'How soon before you finish the house?' he asked once they were inside.

Cara put her bag down and ran a hand through her hair.

'A week,' she said. 'Maybe two. I'll leave after that.'

'You're not leaving.'

She stared at him across the small distance between them.

'I have to leave,' she said. 'This isn't working, Byron. Surely you can see that?'

'I see it, but I don't feel it,' he said, reaching for her.

She suddenly found herself jammed up against his hard body, her breasts tight against his chest, her legs weakening at the intimate embrace.

'Byron, no.'

'Cara, yes,' he said, his eyes boring into hers. 'This is all we have left. I want you and you want me. That's all that matters for now.'

A hundred denials came to her mind, but not one of them made the distance to her lips. Instead she opened her mouth to his descending one and was totally lost in the maelstrom of his touch on her flesh. Fire raced along her veins, flicked along her nerves and set her aflame. His touch was a lighted taper to the tinder of her love for him. She had no hope of escaping the onslaught of heat. It totally consumed her, casting her doubts and fears to the furthest reaches of her mind while she basked in the temporary glory of being in his arms.

He carried her to the bedroom and joined her on the huge bed without once breaking his kiss. Her own mouth had turned savage. It assaulted his with an intent that spoke of deep, unanswered longings. Clothes were a barrier soon dispensed with. Cara heard whimpering cries and realised with a start of surprise that they were her own. Thin wails of pleasure panted from her mouth as Byron caressed every inch of her body, bringing her to a place of intense ecstasy that surpassed all that had gone before. Her body ached for him with an emptiness only he could fill. He filled it with a deep thrust of his aroused body that sent her slim form back into the mattress with a deep sigh of relief. At last he was where she most wanted him!

Byron heard his own garnered breathing. He fought for control, wanting to prolong the intensity of feeling but sure he could not. She totally undid him. She always had. His rigid control shattered under the brush of her lips, the skim

of her hands, the enclosure of her tight body. He felt her
reach the summit and he soon followed, in a tide of pleasure
that pulsed right throughout his body, leaving him spent,
still inside her, his chest heaving against hers, their legs still
entwined, his heart still thudding in the cavity of his chest.

He could feel his eyelids closing on the words he wanted
to say. Her spent body was now curled into his stomach,
the soft curves of her bottom pressing against him intimately, reminding him of all they had shared in the past.
Perhaps it was too late to say what he had to say. They'd
both moved on in their different ways.

Cara didn't seem to need him the way he needed her.
She'd steeled herself against vulnerability, fought to main-
tain her composure, while he was certain, deep down, she
was aching with need just as he ached. He'd tried to fill the
space she'd vacated but it had been a pointless task. No one
came close. No one touched him quite the way she touched
him. He wondered if her vulnerability had connected with
his protectiveness in some sort of strange, elemental way,
marking him as her protector for life. God knew, he wanted
to protect her from the hurt of the past. He wanted to give
her new hope, teach her to believe in herself, in them both,
and embrace what life had to offer.

'Cara?' His voice seemed to fill the silence of the room.

'Mmm?'

'Are you all right?'

'I'm fine.'

'Did I rush you?'

'No.'

'I was in a hurry. You have that effect on me.'

'I was in a hurry too.'

'Making up for lost time?' he asked.

He felt her nod her head against him, even though she
didn't speak. He felt the even pace of her breathing and

knew she had fallen asleep. If only he could do the same so easily. He lay awake with her in his arms, the shifting shadows of night fading to let the early-morning sun anoint their bodies with an incandescent glow.

CHAPTER TWELVE

IT WAS after eight when Cara woke. She opened her eyes to see Byron tying his tie in front of the mirrored wardrobe.

'Hello, sleepyhead,' he greeted her. 'Want to meet me for lunch?'

She sat up and brushed the hair out of her eyes.

'I'm pretty tied up today,' she said, thinking of the rest of the curtains arriving, as well as the tiler coming to measure the upstairs bathroom.

'What about dinner? About seven?'

Cara chewed her bottom lip.

'I don't think it's such a good idea,' she said. 'I'll be leaving soon and—'

'You're not leaving.'

'Byron, this is crazy. I can't do what you want me to do.'

'Don't worry about that,' he said. 'It's not important now.'

No, she thought. Not since Megan sorted it all out for you.

'It's not going to work,' she said desperately. 'We can't go back.'

'No, but we can go forward.'

'I'm not prepared to do that.'

'Why?' he asked. 'Because you can't allow yourself to be happy?'

'I don't want my happiness to be at the expense of someone else's.'

'No one is going to be compromised by your happiness. No one.'

'What about Megan?'

'I told you before—Megan has nothing to do with this.'

'How can you say that?' she asked. 'Don't you care about her at all?'

'Of course I do, but only as a brother should. She's been a part of my life since the year dot.'

Cara examined his expression closely. She wanted to believe him, but how could she—knowing what she knew? It suddenly occurred to her that perhaps he wasn't aware of Megan's pregnancy. But why wouldn't Megan have told him? Surely it would be the one thing that would drive a permanent wedge between her and Byron? She didn't understand Megan's motivation for not using it—as trump cards went it was surely the biggest anyone could want.

'How many times have you slept with her?' The words spilled from her mouth before she could stop them.

Byron glared at her crossly as he shrugged himself into his suit jacket.

'What sort of question is that?'

'A perfectly reasonable one, I would've thought.'

'Quite frankly, I can't see the point in answering it. You didn't believe me before; you're even less likely to believe me now.'

'Try me.'

'I haven't slept with her at all.'

Cara couldn't quite disguise the disbelief in her eyes and he shook his head in frustration.

'I told you it was pointless.'

'But I heard that…' Her words fell away as she ran her mind back over what she'd overheard in the corridor at the Rockcliffe home.

'You hear what you want to hear and the rest you make up, with that martyred mindset you insist on adopting,' he interjected, his tone laced with irritation.

'But surely you must—?'

'Stop it, Cara,' he said heavily. 'This discussion is now

closed. I'm late as it is, and the traffic will be horrendous by now. I'll call you later.'

She opened her mouth to speak but he'd already turned and left the room. She listened as his car drove away a short time after. She could almost see his long, lean fingers tight against the wheel in frustration, lines of tension running along his mouth as he concentrated on getting to work.

She threw back the bedcovers and headed for the shower, the inner muscles of her body protesting slightly at the sudden movement, reminding her with a sharp pang of the pleasure she'd felt in his arms the night before. The hot stinging needles of water hit her body relentlessly and she shut her eyes and let her face receive the cascading spray.

After the curtains had arrived and the tiler had been and gone Cara went for a long walk along the tree-shaded streets. She tried to imagine what it would be like to be secure enough to trust what Byron said instead of doubting him at every turn. Could it be possible that what she had overheard was wrong? That what had been exchanged between the nameless, faceless guests at the party had been nothing more than idle gossip, something to pass the time before the next drink was served? The more she thought about it, the more she had to admit Megan could have any number of lovers; she was popular and attractive and very confident. She was at ease in male company, unlike herself, who still found it hard to understand Byron's physical attraction to her after all this time.

Cara's own attraction towards him was easy to explain— she loved him and had never stopped doing so. He'd told her he no longer felt anything for her that first day when she'd gone to his office. She knew it was different for men, they could disassociate their physical feelings from their emotions, but she couldn't quite quell the faint hope that in some deep place inside he still held some sort of feeling for her.

She thought about Fliss's observations of her behaviour. *Did* she deliberately sabotage her own happiness in some deeply subconscious way because she didn't feel entitled to it? *Was* she punishing herself just as her mother had done?

She sat on a harbourside rock and watched the boats drift past, their sails billowing in the wind like white doves. Time passed and still she sat and listened to the sounds around her, the playful sea breeze lifting her hair occasionally, the sun gradually sinking in the west in a red-golden glow.

'I was wondering where you'd got to.'

Cara was jolted out of her silent reverie by the sound of Byron's deep voice behind her. She got up from the rock and dusted off her linen trousers without meeting his eyes.

'I've been looking for you for over two hours,' he said when she didn't speak.

'I'm sorry.' Her eyes skirted past his as she reached for her sunglasses on the rock. 'I didn't realise the time.'

'Fliss was rushed to hospital just after four this afternoon. I thought you might like to know.'

'Is she…all right?' She looked up at him, her expression full of concern.

'Mother and baby doing well.' He gave her a smile that tore at the fabric of her heart. 'A daughter in somewhat of a hurry, seven pounds three ounces, with jet-black hair and a very determined Rockcliffe chin—or so I'm told.'

Cara met his eyes, her heart thudding heavily in her chest.

'What have they called her?' she asked with a hollow feeling settling in her stomach.

'Emma,' he said proudly. 'Emma Rose Millicent. I think the Millicent was put in to butter up Great-Aunt Milly.'

Byron suddenly frowned as he saw the tortured expression on Cara's face. Tears were falling from her hazel eyes, scoring track marks down her cheeks, and yet no sound of crying came from her.

'Cara?' He touched her on the arm. 'Are you OK?'

She started to cry then. Great hulking sobs that tore at him deep inside. He couldn't remember the last time he'd seen her really cry. She wasn't like Fliss, who bawled hysterically at soppy movies and even cutesy advertisements, especially ones with puppies or kittens. Cara always sat still and silently, as if she were completely detached from her emotions. It had intrigued him at first, and then it had annoyed him that she blocked so much feeling from her life. For in doing so she barricaded him off as well.

'Cara, honey.' He put his arms around her, drawing her sobbing frame into his solid warmth. 'Hey, what did I say to upset you?'

She shook her head against his chest, unable to speak. He stroked the back of her silky head, cupping her neck with his palm. He didn't know what else to do. The evening light was fading and he was standing with his ex-wife in his arms in a state of distress he'd never in his life witnessed before. Fliss's howling over romantic comedies was nothing to this.

Gradually the deep sobs faded to hiccups and sniffles, which precipitated the emergence of his clean white handkerchief. He watched as she buried her face in it, and was surprised by the rush of emotion he felt.

'Let's go home,' he said gently.

He led her back along the track to the street above, her hand totally encased in his. For once she didn't pull away. He felt her fingers grip his, ever so slightly, and smiled to himself; perhaps she was beginning to trust him at long last.

When they got back to the house he led her to the big bathroom upstairs and ran a deep bath. She stood silently as he began to undress her, lifting her arms above her head like a child as he removed her top. Her face bore the ravages of her bout of crying but to him she looked beautiful. She looked like a real person instead of the cardboard cut-out that had annoyed him so much in the past. He felt as if he could reach out and touch her soul, so vulnerable was she. And he wondered then if she could learn to love him the way he loved her. Could she learn to trust him? Would she ever have the courage to tell him about her decision to end her pregnancy? The reasons for it, why she'd done what she'd done, even if he himself could never really understand or accept it.

He'd hated her for it when he'd found out. A business acquaintance had mentioned he'd seen Cara in Sydney, informing him of her very obvious pregnancy. Byron had still been agonising over how to confront her about it when his business associate had called again and told him he'd seen Cara once more, but she was no longer pregnant and there was no pram in sight. He hadn't believed it at first, *couldn't* believe it, but then he'd recalled all the arguments they'd had about starting a family. In the end he had called her, just the once, but her mother had answered the telephone and before he'd been able to stop himself he'd asked if it were true. Edna Gillem had informed him that his child had been dispensed with and he had no business contacting her daughter any more.

He hadn't bothered to contact Cara after that. Instead he'd got shamefully drunk and ended up having a one-night stand which he still hated to think about.

He helped Cara step into the warm water and wondered if she regretted it now, if that was what her weeping was about. The news of Fliss's baby had been the trigger, but why? Cara had always claimed never to want children, and yet seeing her interact with his nieces and nephews had made him wonder if she was being entirely honest with herself.

'I'll go and rustle up something to eat,' he said, running a hand through his hair as he looked down at her.

She didn't answer.

'Cara?'

She looked up at him, her eyes still red-rimmed and swollen.

'Byron, I...' She ran her tongue across her dry lips and began again. 'Could I just go to bed?'

His frown was one of concern.

'You're not hungry?'

'I'm tired,' she said, and reached for a towel.

He handed it to her and without hesitation wrapped it around her and began drying her.

'You don't have to do that,' she said as her hand touched his.

He stilled the movements of his hands as he looked into her eyes.

'If I don't do it I might be tempted to do something else instead,' he confessed ruefully.

'I wouldn't mind,' she answered quietly, her eyes never once leaving his.

He looked at her in mild surprise.

'Are you saying what I think you're saying?'

She nodded.

'Now?' he asked. 'Right now?'

She nodded again.

He touched her cheek with one finger, trailing it down to trace the outline of her soft mouth. She opened her mouth on his finger and the tug of her teeth sent arrows of sensation straight to his groin. She stepped into his arms and he crushed her to him, breathing in the scent of her.

He carried her to the bedroom. He watched her following the movements of his hands as he removed his clothes and desire kicked him deep in his gut.

She didn't say a word. Her hands and mouth spoke for her. Byron relished in her display of feeling. It might not

be love but she wanted him, and that would have to do
for now.

Cara sent her hands on a journey of exploration. She
touched Byron's face, outlining each of his features: the
patrician nose, the straight black eyebrows, the lean line of
his chiselled jaw with its sexy masculine shadow which
grazed her fingers in a slight rasp. She trailed over his neck
and shoulders, rediscovering the contours of his muscled
form. She heard his tight intake of breath when her fingers
found the cave of his navel. She dawdled there, tantalisingly
so, knowing he was waiting for her next move with bated
breath. She could see it in his dark, desire-heated eyes as
they followed her. She wriggled down slightly and began to
tiptoe her fingers one by one through the dark trail of hair
arrowing down to where he most ached for her touch. It
made her feel powerful and feminine to be able to have this
effect on him.

'Oh God!' he groaned as her mouth found its target.

She lingered there for as long as she dared, feeling his
control slipping, tasting it on her tongue.

He stilled her movements with his hands on either side
of her head.

'Honey, I can't take much more.'

She looked up at him through the curtain of her eyelashes
and he groaned again, before hauling her up and underneath
him, trapping her with his body.

'Now I've got you,' he said against her mouth. 'It's payback time.'

Cara shivered in reaction to the playful threat in his
words. His mouth took hers in a searing kiss before moving
down her body, lingering over the hardened peaks of her
breasts before travelling further, until she was writhing under the ministrations of his tongue. He let her subside for a
few moments before sliding into her warmth to take her on
another journey of ecstasy.

When it was over Cara lay in the circle of his arms and two tears slipped unchecked past her lashes. Byron felt the moisture on his forearm and gently turned to look down at her. He blotted another spilling tear with the blunt end of one finger, his eyes warm as they held hers.

'I seem to be having the strangest effect on you lately,' he observed.

She bit her lip, and he frowned when a sob broke free.

'Cara?'

She burrowed against his chest and he laid his hand on the back of her head and let her cry. God knew, she had a lot of crying to catch up on, but he hadn't realised how it would impact on him to hear her do so. It tore at him where he didn't want to be torn.

She fell asleep in his arms, and he lay there listening to the soft sound of her breathing, grimacing every time his stomach growled with hunger. After a while she turned. He shook his numb arm back into life and, leaving her undisturbed, carefully moved away and reached for his bathrobe.

She was still soundly asleep when he came back some time later. Her hair flared out on the pillow in strands of gold and brown, her cheeks were still slightly flushed from crying, dark shadows like bruises underscored her closed eyes, and she was clutching a stray pillow to her chest like a shield.

Byron sighed and slipped into the bed beside her, but the fingers of dawn were already beginning to write their morning message on the eastern sky before he finally closed his eyes and slept.

Cara was showered and dressed when he came downstairs, already two hours late for work. She passed him a cup of tea with the ghost of a smile. He took the tea and bent down to drop a swift kiss on her lips.

'You look so amazingly beautiful when you smile.'

She didn't reply, but her smile increased fractionally.

'If you're not doing anything today I thought you might like to help me choose a present for Emma. Can you meet me at the office at lunch—?' Byron stopped.

Cara had stiffened and the smile had fallen from her mouth. Her eyes had lost their earlier warmth and instead had clouded over, effectively shutting him out once more.

'Cara, should we talk about this?'

She shook her head and refilled her cup from the pot.

'I'm busy today,' she said in a dismissive tone. 'You choose something; she's your niece after all.'

He sighed and headed for the cereal bowls, not wishing to press her. He knew there was something significant in the way she was acting whenever Fliss's baby was mentioned, but just what he had no idea. He wondered if she was thinking of the baby she'd terminated.

His baby. God, it still hurt to think of it. He reached for the milk and then changed his mind, shutting the fridge with a snap.

She looked up at him at that, her eyes still shrouded pools of mystery.

'I'm late,' he said. 'Call me if you change your mind.'

'I won't change my mind.'

He hooked up his jacket with one finger and, scooping his car keys with his other hand, said with a tinge of resentment he couldn't quite remove in time, 'No, somehow I guessed that.'

She watched him leave, but no words to bring him back came to her trembling mouth in time. She sighed and turned to stare out over the lush gardens and the harbour glistening in the distance.

It was so quiet at the cemetery.

Even the birds seemed to be toning down their song in a respectful hush. Cara took the longer walk to Emma's grave.

She didn't quite know why she did that, but suspected it was because she didn't want to come face to face with the words inscribed there. They made it all so final. So permanent and painful.

Walking past the other sites was like walking through a faceless crowd. Cara glanced at the names and wondered what the circumstances of their births and deaths had been. Some were so young—not as young as Emma, but far too young all the same. Others were old, and Cara hoped they'd lived a full life and spread love in their wake.

Her steps slowed down as she approached the tiny bronze cherub guarding her daughter's resting place. The flowers she'd left previously had died and curled over, as if spent in grief. She sank to her knees and plucked them out of the sponge one by one, laying them to one side as if they too deserved some final respect.

She carefully unwrapped the pink carnations she'd brought, and the white baby's breath. The faint breeze stirred the tiny buds like air in fragile lungs. It reminded her of Emma's one and only breath, which had begun and ended her life in the space of seconds. The doctors had been so kind, so gentle as they'd handed Emma to her, still coated with the pale, sticky colour of birth.

They'd left Emma with her for hours. They'd said it would help her grieve properly. But somehow she didn't think it had. It had made the loss harder to bear—although she knew deep down she would do the same if she had her time over again.

She wrapped the spent flowers in the paper that had protected the fresh ones and got to her feet. She began to retrace her steps, but stopped when a pair of shiny black shoes came into her line of vision. She stood rigid in shock when her eyes finally travelled upwards to the tall figure of Byron standing there. The sun was behind him, shielding his expression from her.

'Byron...I was...' She clutched the dead flowers in her hands distractedly. 'I was...I was just...'

'Is this where your mother is?' he asked.

Her eyes skittered away from his.

'No.'

There was a stretching silence. A silence so heavy Cara was sure he would hear the erratic thud of her heart in her chest.

'Who is here, Cara?'

She looked at him for a long moment, torn with indecision. Wasn't it enough that she suffered this loss? What point was there in making him share it with her?

'No one.'

He made an impatient sound in the back of his throat.

'So you regularly come here for no other reason than to wander indiscriminately amongst graves?' His tone was unrestrainedly sarcastic.

She swallowed the lump of dread in her throat without responding. He was stepping past her. Panic tightened her chest. He was three strides away from seeing Emma's grave. Just three steps...

Cara stood there, desperately trying to frame words in her head to tell him what she realised now he should have been told from the very first.

Now it was too late.

'Oh, my God,' Byron stared at the bronze cherub in front of him.

Cara shut her eyes and pictured what he was reading.

Emma Grace Felicity Rockcliffe. Born and died on the same day. I will love you for ever, and somewhere, some day, I will find you again and be your mother.

It was so quiet she could hear Byron swallow.

He turned to her then, his dark eyes blank with shock.

'For God's sake why didn't you tell me?' he rasped.

'I...'

'I had a right to know, damn it!'

His anger hit her like a slap.

He thrust a hand through his hair distractedly before adding, 'Why did you let me think you had an abortion?'

Cara looked at the dead flowers still in her hands.

'I felt I deserved that for what I did.'

'I'm not following you,' he said, his frown deepening even further. 'What did you do?'

She lifted her eyes to his.

'It's my fault she died.'

He paused for a moment, trying to get his emotions under some sort of control.

'What happened?'

'I was...I was in an accident. My mother and I were going to a...a clinic.'

'What sort of clinic?'

'An abortion clinic.'

There was a long silence.

'Tell me you weren't going to go through with it,' he said, in a tone she barely recognised.

She took a deep, steadying breath.

'I would never have done that. I just went to get my mother off my back. I was already six months gone, but my mother didn't know that. I was planning to leave her in a few days, but on the way to the appointment a car came from nowhere. I think it ran a red light or something. My mother was severely injured.'

'And you?'

Cara lifted pain-filled eyes to his.

'They couldn't stop the labour in time. She didn't stand much chance after the impact of the crash. She was too tiny. I held her for hours, but...' The flowers she was holding slipped to the ground at her feet as she buried her head in her hands.

Byron took a deep breath and pulled her into his arms, his eyes settling on his daughter's name over the top of Cara's head.

'I couldn't get away,' she said into his chest. 'I felt so guilty, and my mother played on that guilt until I practically gave up my life to look after her. If it hadn't been for Trevor and the business I wouldn't have survived.'

Byron blinked away the moisture from his own eyes and tried to understand. Why hadn't she come to him? Had she hated him that much?

'She had your mouth,' Cara said brokenly. 'And...and your chin.'

He let her talk it out, not trusting himself to speak. He felt poleaxed. As if someone had kicked him in the gut so hard he could scarcely breathe without pain.

'How did you find me?' Cara asked after a long silence.

'I came home at lunchtime and I saw you at the bus stop. I decided to follow you. I thought you were coming here to visit your mother, although I couldn't imagine why you'd want to after all she'd done.'

He wondered if he should tell her about the phone conversation he'd had with Edna. He decided against it. Cara had enough to deal with; she didn't need any more pain right now.

After a time they made their way out, to where he had parked his car. Neither of them spoke much on the journey home. Byron glanced at Cara several times, but she was looking out of the window with a faraway look in her eyes. He wondered if she was still planning to leave him. He didn't want to force her to stay if she no longer cared for him, but neither did he want to spend the rest of his life missing her, aching for her presence, her touch, her rare smile.

He waited until they were home before he broached the subject.

'Cara?'

'Yes?'

He studied her uptilted face for a long moment.

'Where do we go from here?' he asked.

'Go?'

'Our relationship,' he said. 'Do we have a future together or is it over?'

He could see the answer in her eyes and wished he could stop her from saying it, but he could see it was already too late.

'It's over, Byron.'

'Why?' He was proud of the way his tone was unaffected by the emotion he was feeling inside.

'Because we have no future, only a past.'

'We can make a future. Surely that's possible?'

'No.' She turned away, unable to look him in the eyes. 'I'm afraid that isn't possible.'

'Why, for God's sake?' Desperation was creeping back into his tone and he tried to bank it down. 'Why can't we give it a try?'

She looked at him with a cold blankness in her eyes that totally unnerved him.

'I can't give you what you want.'

'What do you mean?'

'You want children, don't you?'

'Eventually. But we don't have to be in any hurry. We can wait until you're ready and—'

'I'll never be ready.'

'Cara, of course you will be—once you get over Emma. We both need time to heal.'

'You don't understand.' A tiny crack began to appear in her composure.

'Understand what?' he asked. 'I said we'll give it some time. Take all the time you need.'

'Byron you're not listening to me.'

He stopped, somehow sensing she had something serious to say. If only he'd known how serious he might have better prepared himself.

'I was also injured in the accident,' she said, in a flat, emotionless tone. 'I can no longer have children.'

CHAPTER THIRTEEN

HE DIDN'T trust himself to speak. He couldn't speak. Emotion had clogged his throat as he recalled the way he'd forced her back into his life. He cringed at the pain he'd caused her, insisting on things he had no right insisting on, when all the time she had been trying to heal herself. He'd come rampaging through and reopened all her wounds.

'I realise this must be a shock to you,' she was saying. 'I wanted to tell you, but I couldn't do that without telling you about...about Emma.'

Her slight hesitation over their daughter's name tightened his chest another notch.

'You'd end up hating me more than you do now,' she continued. 'You deserve better than that. You'd make a great father. Don't throw yourself away on me, because even if I wanted to I can't give you what you want.'

'We can adopt.' He clutched at the nearest straw.

'No. You can still have your own children. Why shouldn't you do so?'

He didn't have an answer for that. He needed some space to think. Everything that had happened today had completely thrown him. He wasn't used to being so out of control.

'Why did you agree to live with me?' he asked when his thoughts had reshuffled a bit more. 'If you knew all the time you couldn't have another child, why let me railroad you into a relationship with me?'

She found it hard to meet his questioning gaze.

'I felt guilty about the way I'd neglected the business. I

168

didn't want Trevor to lose everything he'd invested just because I'd been preoccupied and out of focus. Besides,' she added with a hint of wryness, 'I thought you'd soon get tired of me when I failed to produce the goods.'

'And the Pill?' His eyes had narrowed and his frown deepened. 'Why bother taking it if you don't really need it?'

'I need it to regulate my cycle. Ever since…Emma…' Her stumble over their daughter's name clawed at him again. 'It's got out of whack; my GP thought a low-dose pill would help.'

He met her eyes across the short distance between them, his expression determined.

'I want us to get remarried.'

It took her a full thirty seconds to register his words.

'What?'

He closed the distance and took both her hands in his.

'I want us to get married right away and start again,' he stated.

'Are you completely mad?' She gaped at him. 'I can't have children! Didn't you hear what I said? I can't give you what you want!'

'I want children, but I want you more.'

She opened and closed her mouth, trying to find the words to answer him but nothing came out.

'There are hundreds of abandoned children in the world we can adopt or sponsor,' he added before she could respond. 'Children are children, no matter who they belong to biologically. I can see that now, after the way you were with my nieces and nephews. You're a born mother; no child you come into contact with could resist you. Damn it, *I* can't resist you—and I'm an adult, although I haven't been acting like one lately. Can you forgive me?'

'I don't know what to say…' She was having trouble

keeping up with him. Her emotions were rocketing around her chest as if they threatened to break through the barrier of her ribcage.

'I want to spend the rest of my life with you, Cara,' he said. 'Surely by now you realise that?'

'You...' She swallowed the lump in her throat and raised her eyes to his. 'You...care for me?'

'I more than care for you. I've never stopped loving you. The day you walked out of my life I wanted to die. I threw myself into my work to compensate, but even after seven years it's just not enough. I want you to fill the emptiness of my life. Only you.'

'I still don't know what to say.' She felt his arms gather her to him, felt herself melt into the solid warmth of his frame.

'What you're supposed to say is you feel exactly the same way,' he said with a soft smile.

'I do, I love you, but—'

'But?'

She threw him a troubled glance.

'I want to be with you, but I feel as if in time you'll come to resent me for not being able to be the sort of partner you need.'

'I need you, Cara. I don't want anything else.'

She so wanted to believe him, but how could she be sure?

He lowered his mouth to hers and her doubts were temporarily suspended by the magic of his touch, his very fingers drawing from her the lurking fears with determined strokes that made her flesh sing with delight. But even after the taste of paradise her worries crept back, like seeping damp cracks in the wall of security she so needed around herself...

*   *   *

Byron smiled at her across the table over breakfast the next morning.

'My folks want to know when you're going to make an honest man out of me.'

Cara could feel herself stiffening in reaction.

'You've told your parents about us?'

'Of course I have.' He pushed his cereal bowl aside. 'I rang them first thing this morning. They were delighted with our news.'

She pushed her own breakfast away untouched.

'Why do your family have to know about everything you do?' she asked.

She heard the tinny clatter of his spoon as he placed it inside his bowl.

'They're my family—that's what families are for: to share one's life with,' he said.

'Couldn't we have had just a few days to ourselves before they were in on the secret?'

'Secret?' He stared at her. 'What secret?'

She shifted agitatedly in her seat.

'I wanted to get used to the idea of us being together again before we announced it to all and sundry.'

'My family are hardly all and sundry.'

'Your family are all-consuming. Even Fliss says so.'

'Yeah, well, she would, since she's had her head screwed by Freud and Jung *et al.* For God's sake, Cara, we're together again! What the hell does it matter who knows about it?'

'Have you told Megan?'

His gaze shifted away from hers.

'I didn't think it necessary to do so.'

'Why ever not?'

He got to his feet and his sudden movement sent a splash of untouched coffee over the side of his mug.

'I'm going to work, and when I return I want the Cara I had in my arms last night back here. Got that?'

She threw him a defiant glare.

'Why haven't you told Megan about us?'

He shoved his chair in, sending another shockwave through his coffee.

'I've told you before—Megan has nothing to do with us.'

'She's pregnant, you know,' she said, watching his face like a hawk.

'That's got absolutely nothing to do with me.'

'Hasn't it?'

'How can you ask that?' He stared at her incredulously.

She gave an indifferent shrug.

'I don't know. She might come in useful one day. You could engage her services as a surrogate mother. At least that way you'd be able to add to the Rockcliffe gene pool.'

'I refuse to partake in such a useless conversation,' he said, reaching for his keys. 'You seem determined to bring down the bridge we've built as if you don't want to be happy. What is it with you? You criticise my family, as if they're intent on destroying you, when all they want is for you to be happy.'

'They're your family, not mine.'

'No, Cara, they're *our* family. They did their best to make that clear to you seven years ago, but you rejected them out of hand. They loved you and welcomed you with open arms, but you kept pushing them away. Even now you're pushing them away.'

'I'm not pushing them away. I just feel claustrophobic around them.'

'Only because you can't keep your guard up all the time.'

'What do you mean by that?' she flashed back at him defensively.

'You don't like crowds because you can't keep your tight façade under control. People slip under the barricade and you feel threatened in case they see the real Cara for who she really is.'

'I thought it was just your sister with the psychologist's degree?' she tossed at him with heavy sarcasm.

'I'm not going to let you get away with it you know,' he said. 'I love you too much to stand by and watch you sabotage your life again. I realise my family are a touch overpowering, especially to someone like you who has missed out on so much of what makes a family a family.'

'I don't want your pity.'

'I'm not giving it,' he said. 'I'm simply stating a fact—we had completely different childhoods, but that doesn't mean we can't have a happy and satisfying life together.'

Cara wanted to believe him, but there was a part of her that kept holding something back just in case.

'Look, sweetheart.' He gave a deep sigh of resignation. 'Maybe you're right; I do allow my family too much space in our lives. Perhaps I shouldn't have insisted on you coming to Melbourne with me.'

Hearing him finally acknowledge it somehow seemed to make his family less of a threat. She knew deep down the problem was really with her. Her childhood experiences had encroached on their relationship just as much if not more than his large and boisterous family had ever done. The truth was she was jealous. Jealous of the bounty of love his family shared between them—each one looking out for the other, taking an interest, laughing together, crying together.

They represented what she'd always dreamed of having, but instead of joining in she'd made herself feel excluded, deliberately sabotaging his relatives' attempts to draw her into the shelter of their inner warmth. Ironic, really, she thought, that it had taken until now to actually see it.

'We don't have to see them unless you want to,' he said across her thoughts. 'And they don't need to be present at our remarriage. We'll keep that simple and private too.'

'I'd like them to be there,' she said with a faint smile. 'Especially Great-Aunt Milly.'

'Well, then.' Byron laughed. 'I'd better order an extra case of champagne just for her.'

She couldn't stop the spread of her smile over her face as she looked up at him.

'Aren't you going to be late for work?' she asked.

He gave his watch a cursory glance before hauling her into his arms.

'Work can wait,' he said huskily. 'I've got something much more interesting to do.'

Cara watched Byron drive off to work an hour later, her emotions in a state of ambivalence. She wanted to be confident of their future together, but no matter how hard she tried to envisage it the picture in her mind became blurred when she thought of their long-term happiness. At the very core of Byron's being was the desire to have his own child, just as his brothers and sister had done. He wanted a replica of his own childhood family—something she was unable to give him.

She loved him, but was it enough? Would her love be enough to carry them through the long, lonely years of middle age and retirement? What if he decided at the last minute he'd had enough of her and wanted to move on? It was so much easier for men; there was no biological clock ticking away in the background like an atomic bomb waiting for the most devastating moment to go off. Byron could still father a child at any age while she had no further chance. That had been ripped away from her, along with the tiny baby she'd so wanted to bring into the world.

Trevor called her during the emptiness of the afternoon.

'I can't believe what a prima donna she is!' he railed as he described his first morning with Megan at the helm. 'She's been asking for all the business receipts. I don't know where they are, for God's sake.'

Cara couldn't help a twinge of guilt at the frustration in

his tone. She couldn't let him take the total blame for the near collapse of the business.

'Let her do what she has to do, Trevor,' she said. 'I'm sure things will start to look up once all the bookwork is sorted out. I'm sorry I left you with it. I should have helped but—'

'She's a bitch on legs,' Trevor said. 'And she got even worse once her boyfriend arrived.'

Cara's spine instantly tightened.

'Her boyfriend?'

'Haven't you met him?'

'I'm...I'm not sure,' she said uncertainly.

'Married guy, high-profile, all hush-hush.'

'Should I know him?'

'Well, sweetie, you did his house for him.'

Her stomach gave a sickening lurch.

'Not...not...' She just couldn't voice his name.

'Dylan McMillanus.' Trevor interrupted the torture of her mindset. 'You know—that guy who's in that soap opera on Channel Eleven. He's going to be a daddy too, but you didn't hear it from me. My lips are sealed like an express envelope.'

Cara felt faint as relief flooded her veins like a hypnotic drug.

'Are you sure?'

'I heard them talking about it,' he said. 'Well, to tell you the truth half the street would've heard if I hadn't shut the office door in time. He wasn't too happy about the kid— bad publicity, you know, having it off with someone when there's a wife already installed at home.'

'A wife and two kids, if I remember,' Cara said, recalling the actor's beautiful children—a boy and a girl not much older than Byron's nieces Katie and Kirstie.

'Men can be such bastards,' Trevor said disparagingly.

'He didn't do it alone,' she pointed out. 'Perhaps Megan wanted a child?'

'Well, according to the little domestic I overheard that's all she's going to end up with. Dylan McMillanus is not the sort of guy to break up a happy home for the sake of a bit of fun on the side. He offered her a pay-out to keep her mouth shut.' He named a sum that raised Cara's brows.

The conversation shifted to other topics, to Cara's relief. Once she'd hung up the phone, however, the irony of it all hit her with a stomach-clenching jolt. Megan was going to have a child, but no husband, and she, Cara, was going to have a husband and no child. No wonder Megan had been on Byron's tail! She must have known Dylan McMillanus would let her down in the end and in her desperation tried to hook Byron instead, but somehow he'd resisted.

A warm glow of feeling rushed through her at the thought of his determination to repair their relationship—even though he was the one making the bigger sacrifice. How she loved him! And how she had misjudged him!

She couldn't wait for Byron to get home. She tried calling his mobile, but it kept switching straight through to the message service. She kept looking at the clock as the evening drew to a close, but the driveway outside stayed empty and the telephone stubbornly silent.

The clock had finally crawled around to ten p.m. when the phone suddenly rang, startling her so much that she stared at it for several rings before moving across the room to lift the receiver.

'Cara?' Byron's voice spoke over the beeps, indicating it was a long-distance call.

'Byron? Where are you? I've been waiting for—'

'I'm sorry, honey. I tried to ring you several times but the line was engaged. I'm in Melbourne.'

'Melbourne?' Her hand on the receiver tightened. Couldn't he last even one day without flying back to his family?

She heard him sigh, and then in the background the sound of voices in lowered tones.

'My father has had a heart attack,' he said heavily. 'I'm at the hospital. I caught the first flight I could.'

'Is…is he all right?' Somehow she managed to get the question out past the shocked oval of her mouth.

'He is now, but it was touch and go there for a while. He's having bypass surgery later this week.'

'I'm so sorry,' she said. 'Shall I fly down?'

'No.' His tone was definite. 'That won't be necessary. There are already too many of us here as it is. The charge sister has sent each of us packing every chance she gets, but we keep drifting back in to support my mother.'

'She must be so worried.'

'She's being very brave, but I think I might need to stay here for a few days and hold the fort. Would you mind?'

'Of course I don't mind!' she insisted. 'Byron, I wanted to tell you something—'

'Honey, the doctor's just arrived; I've got to go. I'll call you in the morning, OK? Love you.'

'I love—' The phone clicked off before she could finish the sentence she most wanted to say.

She sat despondently on the nearest sofa, her legs folding with shock at Byron's news.

It was hard to imagine his father lying in a hospital bed, having so narrowly brushed past death's door. She knew how sick with worry the whole family would be. Her thoughts flew to Fliss, so recently delivered of a child, hit with such dreadful news. She thought of Byron's mother, her soft face pretending not to be overly concerned for the sake of everyone else when inside she was crumbling. She recalled the conversation she'd had with Jan the day of the party, when she'd told her of the child she'd lost thirty-eight years ago, of the way she'd soldiered on nursing her grief.

She thought of Byron's nieces and nephews, their little faces frightened and uncertain at the hushed voices and silent tears.

Cara realised with a sharp arrow of awareness that she wanted to be with them. She wanted to be in the midst of them to offer her own warmth. She wanted to feel with them, to listen and to console. She wanted to help Byron through this difficult time, to show him how much she loved his family. He was right—they were her family now, the only family she had ever really known.

She reached for the telephone, but the last flight of the evening had already closed. Disappointment ripped through her until she almost felt sick to her stomach with it. She even considering going out to the car and driving all night to get there, but decided against it. She would wait for Byron's call in the morning and tell him of her decision to join him as soon as possible.

When the sun came up she crawled out of the big bed and got to her feet, but suddenly the room began to tilt alarmingly—the Persian rug at her feet swirling before her eyes in a sickening vortex and making her feel as if she were going to be sucked right down into it and disappear into nothingness. She made a futile grab for the bedside lamp, to anchor herself, but it came with her to the floor, splintering into a thousand pieces to lie around her unconscious form...

The telephone was ringing. It was ringing inside her head. No—it was ringing on the bedside table on the other side of the bed, Cara realised as she opened her eyes, trying to make sense of why she was on the floor surrounded by broken pieces of lamp-base.

By the time she got to the phone it had stopped ringing and she wondered if she'd imagined it. Had she fainted?

She'd never fainted in her life! Perhaps it was the shock of Byron's father's illness, she rationalised as she reached for her bathrobe. A sudden wave of nausea tilted her stomach and she flopped back on the bed in case she fell once more.

When she thought it was safe to do so she got to her feet, tested her balance for a moment, and carefully stepped towards the bathroom.

She felt better after a shower, but only just. She couldn't understand why she had to be ill right now, when she wanted to be of help to Byron and his family.

The telephone sounded just as she was reaching for a pair of jeans.

'Cara?' Byron's tone sounded clipped and impatient. 'Where have you been? I've been calling on and off for the last thirty minutes.'

'I...' It was on the tip of her tongue to tell him she'd fainted when she remembered he was already going through enough worry about his father without her adding to it. 'I was having a shower.'

'You can still hear the phone in the shower.'

'I...I had the radio on,' she said quickly. 'How is your father?'

'He's holding on.'

'You sound tired.'

'So do you.'

She smiled ruefully.

'I had a terrible night.'

'I miss you,' he said.

Her heart squeezed in her chest.

'I miss you too.'

There was a small silence.

'I want you to come down,' he said. 'I can't stand to be apart from you—especially now.'

'I'll get on the next flight.'

'You don't mind?' he asked, sounding surprised.

'I want to be there.'

'Cara?'

'Yes?'

She heard him sigh.

'Nothing. It can wait till you get here.'

'I'll be there as soon as I can.'

Cara got up from where she'd been sitting on the bed, but the room rolled until she had no choice but to sit down once more. She took a few deep, steadying breaths and tried again, but as soon as she got to her feet the walls of the bedroom began to close in on her as if they were made of fabric. She sat back down and clutched the edge of the bed to steady herself as she tried to make sense of it. Why this and why now?

Her eyes turned towards the telephone. She needed to see a doctor. A doctor would soon sort this out, tell her if she was imagining it or if indeed she had caught some mysterious sort of bug.

She called the nearest medical practice, but the earliest appointment was at two in the afternoon. She took it, reassuring herself that it still left her plenty of time to catch a flight to Melbourne.

She caught a taxi to the appointment, not trusting her ability to drive, even though her dizziness had eased as the day progressed.

Dr Shelley smiled at her across the desk.

'What seems to be the problem?'

'I fainted this morning,' Cara said, suddenly feeling embarrassed.

'Did you hurt yourself?'

'No, but I need to fly to Melbourne this afternoon and I wanted to make sure nothing was wrong. I've never fainted before.'

'Any other symptoms?' Dr Shelley asked, reaching for the blood pressure cuff.

'I feel a bit sick.'

'Have you vomited?'

Cara shook her head as the doctor pumped up the cuff on her arm.

'I haven't actually been game enough to eat. The thought of food turns my stomach.'

'Your blood pressure is a bit low, but nothing to be worried about.' Dr Shelley undid the cuff and laid her stethoscope down. 'We'll check for pregnancy first, and work our way backwards.'

'Pregnancy?' Cara gasped. 'I can't possibly be pregnant!'

Dr Shelley looked at her across the table.

'No chance at all?'

Cara told her briefly about the accident.

'It's still worth checking. The human body has a weird habit of surprising us at times. You say you've been taking a low-dose pill to regulate your periods?'

Cara nodded.

'Ever missed a dose?'

'Once or twice.'

'Roll up your sleeve and I'll take some blood. Pregnancy test kits are best performed early in the morning. This way we can accurately measure the hormone levels and find out for sure.'

'How soon will it be before I get the results?' Cara asked, sitting on the edge of her seat.

Dr Shelley glanced at the clock on the wall.

'First thing tomorrow.'

'But I was hoping to fly to—'

'Is someone going with you?'

'No.'

'Can it wait until tomorrow?' the doctor asked. 'The blood tests I've run will tell us more. Perhaps you shouldn't travel until you know for sure, just in case it's an infection of some sort.'

Cara left the surgery in a daze. She couldn't bear to harbour the thought of being pregnant in case it proved to be a simple virus after all. Her disappointment would be even more crushing if she were to allow herself to hope even for the next few hours…

'What do you mean, you can't get a flight?' Byron's voice when she called him on his mobile was sharp.

She hated lying, but how could she tell him what she was dealing with until she knew for sure?

'Every flight is fully booked.'

'Every airline?'

'I've tried the two major ones.'

He swore violently. 'Damn it, Cara, I need you here.'

'I want to be there too, but I can't—'

'Are you sure you really want to?' A hint of cynicism entered his tone. 'Maybe you're having second thoughts?'

'Byron, you know I want—'

'I know what you want,' he bit out. 'You want to get out of my life, don't you?'

'Of course I don't!' she protested.

'Then prove it. Come down tonight. Surely they have standby?'

'I'll do my best,' she said, knowing there was no way she was going to leave Sydney without knowing the results of that blood test.

She went back to the surgery the following morning.

'You'd better sit down,' Dr Shelley said as Cara followed her into the office.

'Is it bad?' she asked, instantly imagining some sort of incurable disease.

'Depends on how you look at it.'

'Am I dying?'

Dr Shelley shook her head, her tone lightly teasing when she said, 'No, the pregnancy mortality rate is thankfully very low these days. I think we can safely bring you to term this time around.'

Cara blinked at her vapidly.

'You're pregnant, Cara.' Dr Shelley smiled. 'Only a couple of weeks or so, but very definitely pregnant.'

Cara sat in silent stupefaction. It was a long time before she could speak.

'I'm really pregnant? It's not some sort of mistake?'

Dr Shelley nodded and handed her the pathology form with her blood results.

Cara stared at it, fully expecting it to say something entirely different, but there it was in black and white.

She lifted her astonished face to look at the doctor once more.

'I can't believe it.' Her eyes went back to the results in her shaking hands. 'I was told I was infertile.'

'Who told you?'

Cara thought back to that dreadful time. She'd been so ill and dazed after losing Emma. She was sure one of the registrars had mentioned her internal injuries being so bad that a future pregnancy was out of the question—but then she'd been so out of it after the delivery maybe she'd heard incorrectly. Then she recalled how her mother had insisted what she had heard was indeed true, latching on to it, using it at every opportunity to bring her down even further.

'Not a real woman any more! No one will want you now. You and I are the same—no one wants us.' Her mother's words reverberated inside her head until she finally blocked them out to look at the doctor once more.

'I must have misunderstood. I thought the registrar said I couldn't get pregnant again.'

'Perhaps he meant straight away?' Dr Shelley suggested. 'Your body needed time to recover.'

'Yes.' Cara clutched at the explanation gratefully. 'That's what he must have meant.'

'Come and see me in a month, and we'll organise an ultrasound so you can meet your baby for the first time.'

'Am I safe to fly to Melbourne now?'

Dr Shelley smiled.

'Go home and pack. You can go wherever you want.'

Cara left the surgery as if she was walking on air. She couldn't believe it! She was pregnant with Byron's child! She couldn't wait to see his face when he heard the news. He'd be beside himself with the joy she was already feeling, welling up inside her until she was sure she would burst with it.

She called an airline and booked the next available flight. The operator informed her there wasn't a seat available until seven that evening, but in her state of exhilaration she didn't care—as long as she got there to be with Byron in person when she told him her exciting news.

Once she got back to Cremorne she dragged a suitcase from the top of the wardrobe and began packing, not even bothering to fold a single item, tossing in everything she thought she might need and zipping it up with fingers so shaky with emotion she had to make three attempts to secure the overstuffed bag.

She was just hauling it down the last couple of steps of the staircase when the front door suddenly opened and Byron stood there, his expression thunderous as the door shut behind him with an ominous clunk.

'Going somewhere?' His voice cut through the air like knives.

'Byron!' She took the last step towards him, but the bag caught behind her, the zip straining as it dragged against the banister before it finally gave up the fight and the contents burst forth to land haphazardly around his feet.

His eyes ran over what appeared to be the entire contents of her wardrobe before returning to laser hers.

'I thought as much.' He kicked a lacy pair of her panties from his shiny black leather encased foot with such disdain that Cara's heart missed a beat. 'I thought this was what you'd be up to: running away again while my back is turned.'

She opened her mouth, but shock had rendered her speechless.

'I suppose this is a payback for me going to be with my family?' His lip curled.

'I...' She swallowed to clear the blockage in her throat. 'Byron, it's not what you think. I was—'

'Don't insult me with your pathetic lies!' he shouted at her. 'Have you learned nothing after seven years? You can't run away from every little obstacle that gets thrown across your path. You have to face life head on, take it by both hands and live!'

He raked a hand through his already ruffled hair, his voice going down several notches as if in defeat.

'I've done all I can to reassure you, but it's not enough. I love you, and want to spend the rest of my life proving that to you, but you won't give me a chance. I've told you Megan is nothing to me. She's been having an affair with a married man. Apparently she's been using me as a smoke-screen, but I'm afraid I wasn't aware of it until Fliss practically hit me over the head with it. As for my family—I've already told you I won't force them down your throat any more. I respect your need for space and I will do my best to ensure you get it.'

Cara stepped on her very best white blouse to stand in front of him.

'But what about when we need a babysitter?' she asked. 'Aren't extended families really good at that sort of thing?'

He stared at her silently for a full thirty seconds.

'I'm sorry.' He shook his head, as if he wasn't sure he was hearing correctly. 'I think I missed something there. Run that by me one more time.'

She slipped her arms up around his neck, nestling her body against the warm shelter of his.

'I'm pregnant.'

Byron felt as if someone had knocked the air out of his lungs. He sucked in a much needed breath and held Cara away from him, to stare down at her incredulously.

'You're joking, right?'

She shook her head and, reaching into the back pocket of her jeans, handed him the blood test results.

She could see his eyes watering as he scanned the information there, and her heart swelled until she was sure it was going to take up far too much room in her chest.

'There must be some mistake...' His voice trailed off.

Cara couldn't help giggling.

'So far you've said just about everything I said to the doctor this morning.'

'This morning?' He let the blood results float to the floor as he gathered her closer. 'You only found out this morning?'

'That's why I couldn't fly down yesterday. I wasn't feeling well, and the doctor thought it best if I waited until I knew for sure.'

'Why didn't you tell me on the phone?'

'I didn't want to get our hopes up. I was certain the doctors had told me I couldn't have another child.' She told him of her mother's role in overplaying what she'd thought the doctor had said, and how she had accepted it unquestioningly, thinking it was her punishment for not having taken greater care.

Byron held her close as she recalled that painful time, his eyes smarting with the effort of containing himself.

'Besides,' she said lifting her head to look up at him, 'I

didn't want to miss out on seeing your face when I told you.'

'Was it worth the wait?' he asked, his smile wide.

She gave him a rapturous smile as she pressed herself even closer.

'It was definitely worth the wait.'

He kissed her lingeringly before lifting his head to gaze down at her.

'I was so sure you were running away again. I had myself convinced of it. I called and called, and when you didn't answer I knew I had to fly back and find out for sure. When I saw you dragging that case down the stairs I lost it.'

Cara smiled forgivingly.

'I didn't know what to pack, so I packed everything. I was so excited I couldn't think straight.'

Byron gave the skirt he was standing on a rueful look.

'Just as well you won't be needing any of your clothes right now.'

'I won't?' Her eyes began to sparkle as she saw the dark glint in his.

He gave her a sexy grin as he scooped her up in his arms.

'No, you most definitely will not,' he said, and carried her back up the stairs.

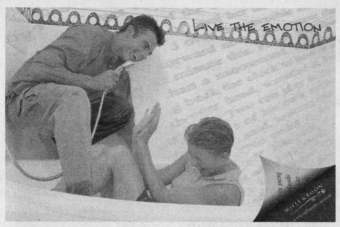
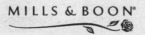

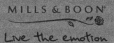

Modern Romance™

THE SPANIARD'S BABY BARGAIN *by Helen Bianchin*

Billionaire Manolo de Guardo has been dumped – by his nanny! He needs a new carer for his daughter...fast! Ariane Celeste is a Sydney reporter sent to interview him, and she's persuaded to help out – temporarily. But Manolo knows a good deal – and he wants to keep Ariane...

IN THE ITALIAN'S BED *by Anne Mather*

Tess Daniels' new job in Italy starts badly when wealthy vineyard owner Rafe di Castelli accuses her of the disappearance of his son. It's actually Tess's sister's fault – but she's missing too. The situation is hard enough without the incredible sexual tension growing between them...

THE GREEK'S ROYAL MISTRESS *by Jane Porter*

When Princess Chantal Thibaudet is helped from the wreckage of her plane by her bodyguard, Demetrius, he insists that she go to his private Greek island, where he can protect her. Being so close to this arrogant commoner is enough to make Chantal throw her royal duty to the winds...

THE SOCIETY BRIDE *by Fiona Hood-Stewart*

Ramon Villalba is handsome, gifted and rich – why would he want a marriage of convenience? Nena Carvajal is a beautiful young heiress who needs protection. It would be no hardship for Ramon to enjoy the pleasures of marriage with Nena, but she expects to marry for love...

On sale 2nd July 2004

Available at most branches of WHSmith, Tesco, Martins, Borders, Eason, Sainsbury's and all good paperback bookshops.

0604/01a

MILLS & BOON

Volume 1 on sale from 2nd July 2004

Lynne Graham

International Playboys

The Veranchetti Marriage

Watch out for this seductive 12 book collection from bestselling author Lynne Graham.

Start collecting now with Volume One on sale from 2nd July 2004.

Available at most branches of WHSmith, Tesco, Martins, Borders, Eason, Sainsbury's and all good paperback bookshops.

FREE
4 BOOKS
AND A SURPRISE GIFT!

We would like to take this opportunity to thank you for reading this Mills & Boon® book by offering you the chance to take FOUR more specially selected titles from the Modern Romance™ series absolutely FREE! We're also making this offer to introduce you to the benefits of the Reader Service™ —

★ FREE home delivery
★ FREE monthly Newsletter
★ FREE gifts and competitions
★ Exclusive Reader Service discount
★ Books available before they're in the shops

Accepting these FREE books and gift places you under no obligation to buy; you may cancel at any time, even after receiving your free shipment. Simply complete your details below and return the entire page to the address below. *You don't even need a stamp!*

YES! Please send me 4 free Modern Romance™ books and a surprise gift. I understand that unless you hear from me, I will receive 6 superb new titles every month for just £2.69 each, postage and packing free. I am under no obligation to purchase any books and may cancel my subscription at any time. The free books and gift will be mine to keep in any case.

P4ZEF

Ms/Mrs/Miss/Mr ....Initials ....
BLOCK CAPITALS PLEASE

Surname ....

Address ....

....

....Postcode ....

Send this whole page to:
UK: FREEPOST CN81, Croydon, CR9 3WZ
EIRE: PO Box 4546, Kilcock, County Kildare (stamp required)

Offer valid in UK and Eire only and not available to current Reader Service subscribers to this series. We reserve the right to refuse an application and applicants must be aged 18 years or over. Only one application per household. Terms and prices subject to change without notice. Offer expires 30th September 2004. As a result of this application, you may receive offers from Harlequin Mills & Boon and other carefully selected companies. If you would prefer not to share in this opportunity please write to The Data Manager at PO Box 676, Richmond, TW9 1WU.

Mills & Boon® is a registered trademark owned by Harlequin Mills & Boon Limited.
Modern Romance™ is being used as a trademark.
The Reader Service™ is being used as a trademark.